JUST FOR YOU, SIR

LAYLAH ROBERTS

Laylah Roberts

Just for you, Sir.

© 2014, Laylah Roberts

Laylah.roberts@gmail.com

laylahroberts.com

ALL RIGHTS RESERVED. This book contains material protected under International and Federal Copyright Laws and Treaties. Any unauthorized reprint or use of this material is prohibited. No part of this book may be reproduced or transmitted in any form or by any means, electronic or mechanical, including photocopying, recording, or by any information storage and retrieval system without express written permission from the author / publisher.

Editor: Khriste Close

Cover Design: Erin Dameron-Hill

❀ Created with Vellum

LET'S KEEP IN TOUCH!

For deleted scenes, early previews and competitions sign up to my newsletter http://eepurl.com/bxulmn

BOOKS BY LAYLAH ROBERTS

Doms of Decadence

Just for You, Sir

Forever Yours, Sir

For the Love of Sir

Sinfully Yours, Sir

Make me, Sir

A Taste of Sir

To Save Sir

Sir's Redemption

Men of Orion

Worlds Apart

Cavan Gang

Rectify

Redemption

Redemption Valley

Audra's Awakening

Old-Fashioned Series

An Old-Fashioned Man

Two Old-Fashioned Men

Her Old-Fashioned Husband

Her Old-Fashioned Boss

His Old-Fashioned Love

Haven, Texas Series

Lila's Loves

Laken's Surrender

Saving Savannah (coming August/Sept 2017)

WildeSide

Wilde

Sinclair

Luke

1

When had paddling a sub's ass become a chore?

Derrick struggled to keep his boredom hidden. The sub tied to the spanking bench deserved his full attention. Anything less was an insult.

"How are you doing, Tara?" he asked, putting the paddle aside.

"I'm good, Sir," she murmured, letting out a soft sigh as he ran his hand over her bottom.

He smacked one of his hands against butt. "Give me a color, sub," he said in a low voice.

"Sorry, Sir. Green, Sir."

Usually, the sight of a sub tied down awaiting his pleasure would have his cock hard and throbbing. But he barely felt a stirring as he rubbed her ass. Moving to the small table that held a number of toys, he picked up a Hitachi wand. The cord was extra-long, easily reaching the bench he had Tara secured to.

Derrick parted her labia and ran the wand over her plump, pink lips. Tara let out a low cry, her body shuddering. She was slick with need, and he knew she was close to the edge.

But he wanted to push her. Just slightly.

"Wait for permission to come," he ordered.

"Oh, oh, please, Sir," she begged.

"You can do better than that," he said sternly, holding the large head of the wand over her engorged clit. She shuddered, her whole body writhing. Sweat coated her naked body.

"Please, Sir. Let me come."

"Not yet."

"Ohhhh."

He actually felt a small spurt of amusement, imagining the names she was calling him in her head. As her breathing grew quicker, her hips thrusting up as far as they could, he knew she was near the end of her endurance.

"Please, Sir. Please, let me come. I need it so bad. Please."

"You may come."

Seconds passed and then she exploded, rocking against the bench, moisture coating the wand. Derrick held the vibrating head against her pussy, dragging the orgasm out before pulling the head away. He placed the wand down then turned back to find Tara lying limp against the bench.

He pulled back her long hair. "Okay, sub?"

She nodded. "Yes, Sir." She opened her eyes to stare up at him dreamily. "Thank you, Sir."

"You're welcome."

He undid her bonds, wishing he felt more for her than slight affection. Tara was one of the waitresses at Club Decadence, and since moving to Austin, Decadence had become a second home to him. Tara would be the perfect sub for him. He could keep his heart out of their relationship while giving her everything she needed.

But he'd soon grow bored, and that wasn't fair to her.

He helped her sit up, wrapping a blanket around her shoulders as he cleaned up the area. Around him, the sounds and scents of Decadence started to filter in. Tara kept her eyes lowered respectfully.

"Master Derrick?" Tara queried as he handed her a bottle of water and a small square of chocolate.

"Yes, Tara."

"Is there something I can do for you? I mean, you gave me such pleasure that I would like to return it."

He cupped her chin, raising her face. "Your job is to do exactly as I say, that pleases me. Understand?"

She nodded, disappointment filling her eyes and he felt like an asshole. Sighing, he rubbed her shoulders. "Want me to find you another Dom?"

Tara shook her head. "No, thank you, Sir. Its busy tonight, I should go help Tilly."

He frowned slightly at the fatigue in her voice. She looked a little too pale for him.

"I thought you were finished for the night." All the wait staff at Decadence were submissives. They could play after their shift was over or on their night off.

"I am, Sir. But Tilly could use some help."

"First, I want you to rest," he told her. "Come, I'll find a free sofa, and you can have a lie down."

"I don't need to rest, I have things to do," she countered stubbornly.

He grabbed her chin again, raising her face as he stared down at her. "That wasn't a request, sub; you will immediately get off that bench and follow me."

Swallowing heavily, she dropped her gaze immediately. "Yes, Sir. Sorry, Sir."

That was better.

Derrick turned away, not looking back. When he found a free sofa in a quiet area of the club, he made her lie down then he spread the blanket over her.

"I'm going to get you a drink," he told her. Something with sugar. "Do not move."

He strode over to the nearby bar where two of the other regular Doms, Alex, and Dylan stood chatting. Dylan, who was an ex-marine and built like a tank, ran the club. Alex, a soft-spoken man with a backbone of steel, looked after the staff.

The bartender, James, was pouring a drink for a Domme at the other end of the bar.

"Everything okay?" Alex asked. He was the ideal Dom to take care of the subs who worked in the club, he had endless patience, but he knew when to push.

"Yeah, Tara just looks a bit pale for my liking. She wanted to go back to work. I want her to rest for a bit."

Alex frowned. "I'll take her some orange juice and check if she's okay."

Dylan nodded, his gaze caught on Tilly, a pleasantly curvy, shy sub, who was currently cleaning tables; her shoulders slumped and head down.

Alex sighed as he picked up the glass of juice. "You'll take care of whatever is going on with Tilly?" he asked Dylan, who nodded.

As Alex passed Tilly, he stopped and bent his head to quickly speak to her. Tilly glanced over at the bar then nodded and walked over to them.

"Master Alex said you wanted to speak to me, Sir?" she asked, standing in front of Dylan, her gaze on the ground.

Dylan was quiet for a long moment. Tilly shifted her weight from one foot to another then stopped abruptly as if realizing what she was doing.

"Tilly, is something wrong?"

"No, Sir," she replied quickly.

Derrick let a smile slip. The little sub was not a good liar. Every inch of her body screamed that something was upsetting her.

He settled back on a barstool to watch. The bartender handed him a whiskey. Although he never drank before a scene, he often enjoyed one after.

"Tilly, tell me what's wrong." Dylan's voice was now pure demand.

"I'm fine."

It was blatantly obvious that she was not fine.

"Look at me," he told her.

She raised her head instantly, and Derrick immediately felt

concerned at the sadness present on the little sub's face. Women brought out his protective instincts, subs even more so.

"Last chance, sugar."

Derrick raised a brow. He'd never known Dylan to give a sub more than one chance. Then he looked down into Tilly's eyes and saw the misery there, and he knew why Dylan was giving the little sub another chance to speak out. They couldn't force her to talk, but like Derrick, it was part of Dylan's make-up to want to help others.

"Just leave me alone. You're not my damn father. Can't I have any privacy?" she snapped.

Wrong answer, little girl. Derrick shook his head.

Dylan's gaze hardened. "Take off your top."

She was wearing a loose, sleeveless top and short skirt. Tilly gaped at Dylan, her jaw dropping open. From what Derrick knew, this particular sub wasn't comfortable being naked.

"You are entitled to your privacy, but instead of being respectful, you chose to snap at me, so now you lose the privilege of wearing your top."

But she pulled off her top without a word, revealing a lacy, red bra. Far racier lingerie than Derrick had assumed would be underneath her rather modest clothing.

"And the bra, Tilly."

She hesitated for a long moment.

"That's five, Tilly," Dylan said. "When I give you an order, I expect obedience."

She raised her gaze, her eyes flashing with defiance, but she quickly lowered them, reaching behind her to unclasp her bra, freeing her breasts.

Reaching out, Dylan cupped both breasts in his hands. Tilly jumped slightly, and Derrick could see the pulse jumping in her neck. But she stood still as Dylan ran his thumbs over her nipples.

"What do you think of these breasts, Master Derrick?" he asked as Tilly's breath quickened, the nubs stiffening and deepening in color.

"Beautiful," Derrick replied, biting back his smile as the little sub glanced up at him with surprised eyes. The girl needed a boost of confidence.

"Aren't they? Full, round and responsive. I think they're missing something, though."

Tilly's worried gaze turned back to Dylan.

"James, hand me my bag," Dylan ordered without taking his gaze from the anxious sub before him.

The quiet bartender handed Dylan his bag of toys. Dylan reached in and pulled out a pair of nipple clamps that were connected with a long, silver chain.

"Give me a little help?" Dylan asked Derrick.

"Certainly," Derrick replied, rising from his stool to step behind the sub. He brushed his chest against her back. She shivered.

"Easy, love," he murmured in her ear as he cupped her full breasts and held them up for Dylan.

Slowly, Dylan placed one clamp over her left nipple then tightened it.

Tilly took in a sharp breath then let it out slowly.

"Okay, Tilly?" he asked.

"Y-yes, Sir."

Dylan placed the other clamp on her right nipple then nodded at Derrick.

Derrick cupped her shoulders, giving them a brief squeeze before moving back to sit at the bar. Dylan tugged on the chain linking the two clamps, and Tilly sucked in her breath, a mix of pleasure and pain filling her face.

There was a small weight attached to the chain. Dylan let the chain go, and the weight caused the clamps to pull at her nipples.

Dylan pulled over a bar stool. "Lean over it, so your stomach rests against the seat."

Tilly nibbled at her lower lip as she lay over the stool. Dylan grabbed her around the waist, lifting her, so her legs were off the ground, her breasts dangling down, and the chain pulling at her nipples.

"Five then. You'll count and ask me for another."

"Yes, Sir."

He lifted up her skirt, revealing lacy, red underwear. Dylan pulled them down below her pale, tense butt cheeks.

Dylan rubbed his hand over her bottom. "Relax," he told her.

Tilly snorted softly. Derrick had to bite back a smile. Glancing over at Dylan, he saw his friend's amusement. But none of it bled into Dylan's voice.

"Something you want to say, sub?" he asked sternly.

"No, Sir," she replied, taking a deep breath and releasing it.

Dylan smacked his hand down on one cheek with a loud crack.

"Ow. One, Sir. May I please have another?" she asked.

Her other butt cheek was given the same treatment. These weren't light little love taps.

"Two, Sir. May I have another, please?"

Dylan continued on. By the fifth smack, Tilly was visibly beginning to relax. Dylan helped her off the bar stool, holding her around the waist until she was steady.

With a gasp, she reached around and quickly pulled her panties up before yanking her skirt down.

Dylan leaned back and grabbed hold on an empty bar tray, handing it to her.

"Back to work, sub," he said gruffly.

Tilly's eyes widened, filled with shocked dismay. "I can't walk around like this!"

Dylan narrowed his gaze. "Excuse me?" he growled.

Immediately, her gaze dropped, her submissive side kicking in.

"I can't walk around like this, Sir," she muttered.

"You can, and you will. Any more protest and I'll decorate more than your nipples, understand?"

Her head shot up, and she bit her lip as she stared at him.

"What do you say?"

"Yes, Sir. Thank you, Sir."

"Go on then, you're already behind in your work."

With a sigh, shoulders slumped, she turned away.

Dylan muttered something under his breath. "Tilly," he said.

She stopped, turning. Dylan stepped up beside her.

"Shoulders back, head up. You're beautiful, sugar. You just need to believe it." He tapped her chin. "When you're ready to talk to me, I'll be here, understand?"

"Yes, Sir. Thank you, Sir."

"Seriously lacking in self-confidence, isn't she?" Derrick asked after she'd walked off.

Dylan frowned. "We're trying to work on that, but it's not easy to break through those defenses she's erected around herself."

Derrick nodded.

"Something going on with you, man?" Dylan asked.

"What makes you ask that?"

"You seem kind of disinterested lately, detached."

He was surprised Dylan had noticed, he thought he'd hidden his feelings better.

"How is Roarke? Haven't seen him in a while," he said, trying to change the subject. Roarke Langdon was an old friend, who owned Club Decadence, along with a number of other BDSM clubs across the state.

Dylan threw him a knowing look but answered anyway. "He's busy settling Ava and Sam into their new place. They bought this huge place just out of the city. I've never seen them happier. It's sickening."

Derrick smiled sadly. "That sort of happiness can be a blessing and a curse."

Dylan raised his eyebrows. "You ever been married?"

"A long time ago. Back home in the UK." He put his glass down, fighting back the old memories. Nothing good would come from them. Although he still lived with the guilt and regrets, it had been nearly twenty years since Cara had been murdered. He'd learned that punishing himself served no purpose. All he could do was make sure he never made the same mistakes again.

"How's Holly?" Dylan asked, thankfully changing the subject.

Derrick smiled. His sister-in-law was the only family he had, and he adored her.

"She's great. She and Brax bought a new place a bit closer to Austin. Brax didn't like her having such a long commute. She drives in three days a week now." Holly had protested the move, but although Brax would indulge her in most areas, her health and safety were things he took very seriously. Brax wasn't just her husband, but her Dom as well. Her well-being was his main priority.

Derrick was grateful that Holly had found a man who would take care of her and who made her happy.

"Alex looks worried," Dylan commented, and Derrick turned his head to see the other man approach, a frown on his face.

"Tara needs to go home," Alex said. "She's exhausted, but she's refusing to admit it."

"I can cover here while you take her home," Dylan offered.

Alex shook his head. "She's refusing to leave with me. Stubborn little brat."

Derrick stood. "I'll take her."

Alex hesitated. "You'll take care of her? She might need someone to stay with her for a bit."

Derrick raised his brows. "Yes, mother, I'll tuck her in and sing her a lullaby." He clapped the other man on the shoulder. "Relax, Alex. I'll look after her. I promise."

"THANKS FOR BRINGING ME HOME, Sir. I'm fine now."

Derrick wasn't so sure. Tara was huddled into a corner of her living room couch, a blanket wrapped around her as she sipped on the hot chocolate he'd made her.

There were dark circles under her eyes, standing out in contrast to her milky-white skin. He looked around the apartment, not liking what he saw. Although she had tried to brighten the place up with some colorful cushions and cheap artwork, there was no disguising how rundown it was.

The walls had peeling wallpaper that looked like it was straight out of the '70s, there was a big hole in the wall behind her head, and the carpet had seen better days.

"I don't like leaving you here. It's not safe."

"It's fine, Sir. I've lived here for two years now."

The neighborhood wasn't the best, but it wasn't a high crime area, either.

"All right," he said reluctantly. "But tomorrow, I'll arrange for better locks on this door and a security system."

"I can't afford that."

"I can. And before you protest, either you take my offer, or I'm going to call Master Alex right now and have him come over. What's it to be?"

Her eyes grew wide. "The security system," she said in a quiet voice.

Yeah, that's what he'd figured.

"Okay. I'm going now. I want to hear you lock up behind me."

Derrick waited until he heard the lock engage before heading down the stairs, and outside into the warm Austin evening.

Fatigue pulled at him as he climbed into his car. He usually had his driver take him to the club, but Robert was away visiting family, so he was on his own.

Pushing past the fatigue, he pulled away from the curb and headed home.

2

The loud screeching of tires woke Jacey from a light sleep. Heart beating frantically, her skin clammy, she glanced around frantically, disorientated. Oh God, she'd sat down on these steps a few hours ago to rest, not intending to fall asleep. So stupid! Another screech caught her attention. Jumping up, she watched a small car spin out of control across the street.

Jacey cringed as the car crashed into a power pole with a sickening crunch. Shock held her immobile for precious seconds. Shaking slightly, she grabbed her backpack and slung it onto her back then ran toward the accident.

The car had rolled onto its roof. Jacey knelt on the pavement to peer into the driver's side. A car door slammed shut, and she glanced up, swallowing nervously as a large man approached. Jacey fought her instinct to turn tail and run.

"What happened?" a deep voice asked. "Are you all right, miss? Miss?" His voice deepened, the demand for obedience clear.

"I'm fine," she said. "I wasn't in the crash."

A low moan drifted out from the car and Jacey sighed in relief. "The driver is alive. We have to help." As she reached for the car door, the man grabbed her hand, pulling her back.

She glanced up at him in surprise.

"We need to get some help," he told her, pulling a cell phone out of his pocket. "We could make the injuries worse."

Of course, what had she been thinking? Jacey nodded. Kneeling carefully on the ground, she peered in the driver's window. "It looks like a woman. She's not moving."

"Here, let me have a look."

She glanced back to find him crouching beside her, a flashlight in his hand.

"Where did that come from?"

"I had it in the boot of my car." He had a slight English accent. Sexy.

Now is really not the time for those sorts of thoughts, Jacey.

She shifted away, and he aimed the flashlight into the car.

"Looks like there is just the driver," he spoke into his phone. "A woman. Can't really see how badly she's hurt."

There was another moan from the driver.

"At least she's alive," Jacey said. "What happens if the car catches on fire?"

Derrick glanced at the car. "I can't see any sparks. If you smell anything burning, let me know. An ambulance should be here soon."

"It feels wrong to just stand here and do nothing for her." Jacey bounced up and down, nervous energy flooding her system.

"I know." He placed his hand on the lower half of his phone. "There's a blanket in the boot of my car, why don't you go get it while I try to open this door. We can try to keep her warm."

Jacey nodded and jumped up, grateful to have something to do. She rushed toward the high end, luxury car parked at the accident scene. Moving around to the still open trunk, or boot as he kept calling it, she quickly grabbed the blanket.

Hurrying back, she saw that he'd managed to get the door open. She was trying to cover the woman without jostling her when she heard sirens in the distance.

DERRICK SLIPPED off his jacket and swung it over the shoulders of the shivering woman standing next to him. The temperature had dropped, but he suspected her tremors were due to adrenaline more than anything else. One of the cops had asked them to stand on the sidewalk near Derrick's car until he could take their statements.

"Oh, I'm okay," she said, trying to pull the jacket off to hand it back.

Derrick laid his hands over hers, stopping her. "Keep it on, you're shivering."

"But you'll get cold," she protested.

He raised a brow. "Your comfort comes first."

Her forehead twisted into a frown. "Why?"

Derrick had only just met her, and already she stirred his protective instincts. There was something about having a woman lean on him that filled an empty place inside him, that made him want to be stronger, a better person.

Slightly built, she seemed delicate and yet he could see the strength in her. She hadn't panicked when she'd come across the accident. Despite her obvious nerves, she'd kept a cool head.

He studied her with a frown. The street light they were standing under pierced the darkness, allowing him a better view. Large eyes stared up from a thin, pale face. Dark, curly hair surrounded her head, giving her an almost pixie-like appearance. She was so tiny, she barely reached the middle of his chest.

How to answer her without sounding like a complete Neanderthal? Had she been Holly or one of the submissives from Decadence, he wouldn't have had to explain himself; they'd have understood his need to look after them.

"Just part of the good manners my mum drummed into me, love. You wouldn't have her ashamed of me by handing my jacket back, would you?" His explanation seemed to work as she snuggled deeper into his jacket. He liked the idea that his scent surrounded her, marking her.

Bloody hell, what was he thinking? He didn't even know her name.

"I'm Jacey, by the way," she said, holding out one hand while trying to keep the jacket on her with the other.

He took her hand in his, holding it for a long moment. "Derrick. It's nice to meet you, Jacey."

"You too." She gave him a puzzled smile as she tugged her hand free.

Derrick glanced around, trying to find something to distract himself from his growing attraction to the tiny woman. The EMTs were loading the driver into the ambulance.

The same policeman who had asked them to wait broke away from his colleagues and walked toward them.

"Sorry to keep you waiting," he said, pulling out a pad and a pen. "I'm Officer Mast. If I could just get a statement from both of you, along with your names and addresses."

"Is the driver going to be okay?" Jacey asked in a quiet voice.

"I believe so, ma'am," the officer answered. "Looks like she banged her head, she'll be bruised and sore for a while, but she should be fine."

"She's bloody lucky, driving around in a sardine can like that," Derrick muttered with a frown, thinking about how small his sister-in-law's car was. He'd never been happy with Holly driving it.

"An expensive sardine can," the officer commented, nodding in agreement. "She is being transported to the hospital, so we just need to piece together what happened. Is that your vehicle?" He nodded over at Derrick's car.

"Yes, it's mine. I'm afraid I didn't see the accident, however. By the time I pulled up, the car was already on its roof."

"And you, miss? Were you together?"

"No, I'm not, we're not." She gave him a nervous look then took a deep breath. "I was passing by, alone, and saw the accident."

"Okay, I'm going to call a colleague over to take your statement, miss. Joe," he called out. "Come over here, will you?"

"Is that okay with you?" Derrick asked Jacey as the two policemen spoke to each other. "I can stay with you if you'd rather." He wouldn't leave her if she was feeling vulnerable or afraid.

She stared up at him for a long moment. "You're an interesting man, Derrick. I have a feeling your wife must be a lucky woman."

"I'm not married," he replied. It should have occurred to him that she might be, though. "Do you need to call anyone? They could come and get you."

Jacey shook her head. "No. There's no one to call." A look of sadness crossed her face before disappearing.

How did someone as beautiful and sweet as Jacey not have anyone worrying about her? Derrick opened his mouth to question her when the officers returned and split them up.

As he was answering Officer Mast's questions, Derrick kept an eye on Jacey. She had her arms folded around her body defensively, and she couldn't seem to meet the officer's gaze. There was something odd going on, but he couldn't figure out what it was.

"Right. Thanks, Mr. Ashdown. I think we have everything we need, but we'll get back to you if we need anything else." Derrick nodded to the officer who became distracted as a van pulled up.

"Didn't take them long," the cop muttered, turning away to intercept the people jumping out of the van, one of them carrying a news camera. What the hell? He turned and strode toward Jacey.

JACEY COULD SCARCELY BELIEVE that she'd just lied to the police, giving them a false name and contact details. But what other choice did she have? She couldn't give them her real name. Nor did she want to tell them that she was homeless. That the reason she'd been first on the scene was because she'd been sleeping in a doorway across the street.

She needed to get out of here. Now.

"Are we finished now?" she asked.

"Yes. Thank you. We'll be in touch if we need more."

Jacey nodded, trying not to look as guilty as she felt. Did he know she was lying? Did he notice that she couldn't meet his gaze?

"Jacey, are you okay?" She jumped, whirling toward Derrick.

"Ahh, yes, I'm fine." She glanced over to find a man pointing the news camera their way. "I'd really like to leave, though."

Derrick glanced around. "Where's your car? I'll walk you to it."

"Excuse me, sir, ma'am, did you see the crash? Did you speak to Cece? How badly hurt was she?"

Derrick turned to frown at the man rushing toward them. A shorter man, carrying the camera, followed quickly behind him.

"Cece? The singer?" Jacey said surprised. "Wow. I didn't even recognize her."

"I'm with Channel 7. Can we interview you?"

Jacey quickly turned her face away, toward Derrick. He placed his arm around her, pulling her tight against him. Immediately she felt safer. Which was crazy, she didn't even know him. He could be a serial killer. It wasn't like she had the best instincts when it came to men, she'd married Stephan after all.

"Unfortunately, we have to get going." Derrick's voice was polite but firm.

As though sensing her discomfort, Derrick ran his hand up and down her back, soothing her.

"Come on, love."

Jacey kept her face turned to his chest as he steered her away and toward his car. He placed an arm around her, sheltering her.

"Where is your car?"

"Umm, I don't have one."

"Then how did you get here?" he asked, stopping next to his car and turning her to face him.

"I was walking."

He stared down at her for a long moment, and she had to force herself not to squirm.

"Walking around alone at night isn't safe, Jacey," he scolded.

She found herself biting back an apology. Wow, he was good.

"You're not my father, you know."

"Sounds like you could use one." He opened the passenger door. "Hop in, I'll drive you home."

"Oh, that's not necessary," she said. "I can walk..." she trailed off at the stern look on his face. "Or maybe not."

She climbed into the car.

3

She was an idiot.

Even children knew not to get into cars with strangers and here she was, sitting on heated, buttery soft leather seats being driven God knows where. What if he was taking her to his house? He could keep her locked up in his basement for years as his sex slave.

Damn it, Jacey, what were you thinking?

She hadn't been thinking. She'd been seduced by his gorgeous face and take-charge attitude. Now she was probably being driven to her final resting place, and all she could think about was how nice it was to have a warm butt.

Hadn't she learned not to trust people? She had more than just herself to worry about now, she had to be more careful. She resisted the urge to rest her hand on her stomach. At ten weeks, she wasn't showing yet, but she didn't want to do anything that might give her secret away.

Jacey frowned as Derrick pulled into the parking lot of an all-night diner.

"What are you doing?" she asked. This wasn't where she'd asked to be dropped off. She'd given him the address of some apartments close to the diner where she worked.

"I don't know about you, but I could use some coffee and pie. Join me?"

Her stomach clenched at the thought. Dinner had consisted of a few dry crackers. Most of her meals were taken at the shelter or whatever she was given at the diner where she worked.

She should refuse. She should just walk away and find somewhere to rest for the night. Not that she'd get much sleep. Not now.

Her stomach rumbled loudly, and she blushed bright red.

"I think that's my answer," he said with amusement.

"Yes, thank you."

Derrick got out of the car. She undid her seatbelt. Reaching down, she grabbed her backpack. It held everything she currently owned in the world. A scary thought if she let herself think about it for too long.

Derrick opened her door. How long had it been since a man had held open a door for her?

Stephan had opened doors for her when they'd been dating when others were watching. She hadn't realized until it was too late that those perfect manners were all for show.

Stupid bitch, all you're good for is sucking my dick.

"Jacey? What's wrong?"

Snapped out of her memory by Derrick's concerned voice, she glanced up at him in surprise. "What? Oh, nothing. Sorry, I was thinking about something else."

"Didn't look like a pleasant thought," he replied, opening the diner door and gesturing her to go in. It was slightly less rundown on the inside, although that wasn't saying much. But it was warm and, while the vinyl seats were worn and the decor hadn't been updated since the eighties, it had a cozy feel.

Jacey sat on one side of a booth as Derrick squeezed himself into the other side. Booths just weren't made for someone of Derrick's height. He sat down, resting an arm along the back of the seat.

"This doesn't seem to be your sort of place," she commented.

It was obvious Derrick had money. His luxurious car, expensive clothing, the way he acted, all pointed to someone who was wealthy. So why would he choose to eat here?

Stephan would never step foot in a place like this, he'd be too worried about dirtying his Armani suit or, Lord forbid, someone seeing him here.

"And what is my sort of place?" he asked, his lips tilting up in amusement. Damn, he took her breath away. He had a lean, muscular build. A few days growth covered his cheeks and chin, his dark brown eyes stared at her.

Her whole body tingled.

Calm down. He might be the sexiest man she'd ever seen, but he was also a stranger. A rich, self-assured stranger. She needed to be more cautious. She couldn't trust him.

She couldn't trust anyone.

"I don't know, maybe a gentleman's club with lots of dark leather sofas and men smoking cigars and sipping expensive whiskey."

He barked out a laugh. "Hate to tell you, love, but I don't smoke cigars nor have I ever been to a gentleman's club."

"Derrick!"

Jacey glanced up in surprise as a waitress, a huge smile on her face, approached them. Derrick smiled up at the plump woman who looked to be in her late forties.

"Alice, how are you?"

"I'm good thanks. How's Holly?"

"She's great. Settling in to her new house," Derrick replied.

Who was Holly?

"Well, tell her I said hi next time you see her." The waitress turned to look at Jacey.

"Alice this is my friend, Jacey."

"Pleased to meet you, Jacey. Can I get you your usual, Derrick?"

"That would be great. Jacey, what would you like?"

"I'll just have coffee, thanks," she replied.

Obviously, he came here a lot, and she felt slightly ashamed of herself for judging Derrick based on his appearance.

Derrick stared at her for a long moment. "Bring us two slices of pie, please, Alice."

Jacey glared at him. "I said I wanted coffee."

He shrugged. "If you can't eat it, then you can take it home."

Jacey took a deep breath, searching for calm. She hated being controlled. Been there. Done that. Never going back.

"So, who's Holly?" Drat, she hadn't meant to ask that.

Derrick's face lightened as he smiled. "Holly is my sister. Well, technically, she's my sister-in-law, although we're closer than that. She also works for me. She just got married a few months ago. Good guy, even if he does live miles away, by Waco."

"You miss her."

He nodded. "She drives in three times a week then works from home the rest of the time."

Alice brought over the coffee and then quickly returned with two huge slices of apple pie. The scent of cinnamon and pastry made Jacey's mouth water and almost before she knew what she was doing, she had scooped some into her mouth. She closed her eyes in pleasure as the tartness of the apples, followed by the rich pastry filled her taste buds.

"Good, right?" Derrick said.

She opened her eyes, blushing slightly as she realized the sight she must have made.

"It's delicious, best I've ever had." Not that she'd eaten a lot of pie in her life. Her mother, then Stephan had kept a close eye on her diet. But they weren't here anymore; Jacey could eat what she liked. And this pie was worth every penny she would be spending on it.

She'd have to check if Jimmy had any spare shifts at the diner. She couldn't work anywhere that needed details like a social security number and address. Jimmy never asked her for any personal details, he paid in cash, and when she worked a shift, she got a free meal.

At the moment, it was the most she could hope for.

"I hope Cece is going to be all right," she said as she pushed the plate away, the slice of pie only half-eaten. She was full.

"Who is Cece and why were those reporters there?"

"You really don't know who she is?" Jacey asked.

He shook his head.

"She's a singer. She's really popular at the moment. You know, she sings that song, *Raven's Heart*?"

He looked at her blankly, so Jacey sang him a few lines.

"That was beautiful."

She nodded. "Cece is a great songwriter."

"No, not the song. Your voice. You have a fantastic voice."

Jacey shrugged, blushing slightly.

"Officer Mast seemed to think she would be fine," Derrick said, finishing off his slice of pie. "I'd like to know what caused her to crash."

"I guess we'll find out tomorrow, it's bound to be all over the news."

"I noticed you didn't want to stick around once the reporters appeared." Derrick leaned back. He sipped slowly on his coffee. "You camera shy?"

"Something like that," she said warily. "I'm kind of tired; do you think we can get going?"

"Sure thing, love. My apologies. I shouldn't be keeping you out so late. I'll get Alice to box the rest of your pie up for you."

He rose and grabbed the plates, surprising her by taking them to the counter. When he returned, he held a small brown box in his hand.

He held out a hand to her, and after a moment's hesitation, she took it. A shiver of pleasure raced through her as he helped her stand.

What was it about him that made her feel so safe yet all jittery at the same time?

"Everything okay?" he asked.

"Umm, yeah. Oh, let me get some cash."

Derrick just placed his hand on her lower back, steering her away. "No need. All taken care of."

"Oh, well, let me pay you back."

"Don't even think about reaching for your wallet. When you're out with me, Jacey, I pay."

"This wasn't a date," she insisted as they stepped outside. Drat, it had grown colder. She was going to have to start getting to the shelter earlier so she could claim a bed. She'd been too late tonight.

Derrick held open the passenger door for her, handing her the box once she had buckled her seatbelt. "I know. But that doesn't matter. When a woman is out with me, I pay. I don't care who they are."

He closed the door and walked around the car, to the driver's side.

"Derrick?" she queried, feeling ungrateful all of a sudden.

"Yes?"

"Thank you. The pie was delicious and just what I needed."

Even in the limited light from the diner, she saw him relax. "You're welcome. It may not have been the most ideal circumstances, but I'm glad I met you, Jacey."

"Me too." Surprisingly enough, she actually meant it.

4

"Ahh, there's my favorite girl," the slimy voice came from behind her. "How you doing, Jacey?"

Jacey hid a shudder, determined to show no reaction. How did he manage to make her name sound like a dirty sex act?

She continued to move down the line, smiling her thanks as the food was portioned out onto her plate. Some days she longed to use some of her cash supply and stay in a motel for the night. Just a cheap one. Somewhere that she could be alone. Where there wasn't a room full of other women, snoring and crying out in their sleep. And where she didn't have to put up with weasels like Ronald hassling her.

Right now, she'd give anything to be back in the diner with Derrick. She just couldn't get him out of her mind, those deep, brown eyes, his sexy voice, and his wide shoulders. How would it feel to have him touch her? Kiss her?

"Aren't you gonna to talk to me? Cat got your tongue? Or is it frozen 'cuz you're such a frigid bitch." That last bit was whispered in her ear.

Ignore him, ignore him.

She turned away, walking over to sit at one of the tables.

Ronald sat next to her, so close that his stench made her gag. And she thought she'd grown used to the smell of unwashed bodies. Her stomach clenched, and she swallowed heavily, fighting back nausea. She placed her hand on her tummy, trying to calm her queasiness. She hadn't had lunch, and she needed to eat. For the baby more than herself. However, it seemed that pregnancy made her more sensitive to smell and Ronald was fast turning her off her food.

"Move away from me. Please." He was just a bully. Don't react and he'll go away.

"Now Jacey, is that any way to speak to a friend?" He leaned in as he spoke to her, running his fingers up her arm. "Play your cards right, and you and I could be very good friends."

There was a thump as someone placed their tray on the table next to Ronald. Jacey glanced away from her food as Cady leaned around Ronald to nod at her. Cady was a regular at the shelter. Small, but tough, she mostly kept to herself. She'd never let anyone push her around.

"You know, Ronnie, you might wanna try a breath mint now and then, because you're literally talking shit," Cady told him before digging into her food.

Quiet laughter rose from the people at the table as Ronald grew purple with rage. He glared at the other people sitting around until they shut up, looking uncomfortable.

"You're gonna regret that, you little bitch," he hissed at Cady.

"Not as much as your mother regretted having you," Cady replied. "If you were twice as smart, you'd still be stupid."

Jacey wished she had a quick mouth like Cady, but she'd been raised not to fight back. To appease rather than confront. And Stephan had only reinforced those lessons. She didn't have a clue how to fight back. Maybe she needed to learn some of Cady's attitude.

Fury lit Ronald's face, making a vein pop out on his forehead as his hands clenched into fists. Her stomach clenched with worry. She felt sure he was about to hit Cady. Everyone else at the table fell quiet, watching.

"Ten more minutes everyone," one of the shelter volunteers called out, breaking the spell.

Ronald stood and giving Cady a last glare, stormed off, leaving his uneaten tray of food behind.

"Waste not, want not." An older man, with a long, gray beard, slid into his seat and started to dig in.

Jacey forced herself to eat. Last time she'd taken a good look in the mirror, she'd noticed how prominent her cheekbones were. The baby needed nutrition, and so did she.

When she was finished, she picked up her tray and carried it to the kitchen window before making her way to the sleeping quarters.

"You've got to stick up for yourself with slime like Ronny boy," Cady said, falling into step beside her.

"I know. But I figured if I ignored him he would just give up."

Cady snorted. "How's that working out for ya?"

"Not great."

"You're different from everyone else here. You're softer, you say please and thank you. You stand out, and being in this place, you don't wanna stand out."

"It's kind of you to worry about me."

Cady let out a frustrated breath. "There you go again. I'm not worried about you. We're not friends. We're not goin' to go out and get manicures and facials and whatever else you used to do with your friends. I'm here to survive, and I'm just tryin' to give you some advice, so you survive too. You need to toughen up."

Jacey stopped, grabbing Cady's arm. "I thought I was doing a pretty good job of surviving." She hadn't fallen into a ball of hopeless despair and just given up.

Not that she hadn't been tempted to.

Cady looked her up and down. "Gotta admit, you've done better than I thought. First time I saw you, I felt sure you weren't gonna last the week. But you got to stick up for yourself. People like Ronny, they don't play by any rules and you can't either."

Jacey thought for a long moment. "You're right. So teach me."

Cady put her hands on her hips. "What am I? A social worker?"

"No, but you're a good person, and you like me."

"We're not friends," Cady repeated as she walked into the

women's sleeping area of the shelter. "And I'm not a good person. You tell anyone otherwise, and I'll have to hurt you."

Jacey let out a small smile. "But you'll help me?"

"Guess someone's got to."

~

Derrick leaned back on the sofa in his living room, tapping his fingers on the arm. Was it possible to be obsessed with a woman after meeting her just once? Derrick was seriously beginning to think there was something wrong with him. He just couldn't stop thinking about a tiny pixie with big brown eyes and a riot of curls.

He hadn't thought about another woman this much since his wife died.

"Derrick? Derrick? Derrick!"

Derrick sat up in his chair, startled to find Holly standing in front of him, hands on her hips as she frowned down at him.

"I'm sorry, love. Did you say something?"

Her forehead creased into a frown as she stared down at him. "I've been calling your name for the last few minutes. What is wrong with you? You've been like this for the last two weeks. One minute you're here, the next you're in another world."

He smiled at her. "Nothing is wrong. I'm just preoccupied. Now, what did you ask me?"

Holly continued to frown, but answered him anyway, "Brax will be here in about forty minutes so I thought I would order some take-out, anything in particular you feel like?"

"Whatever you want is fine with me."

"You sure you're okay with Brax and me staying tonight?" she asked with uncustomary shyness.

Shit. He must really have been acting like an idiot if she had to ask him that. Holly had lived with him for years, and he'd worked hard to convince her that she was in no way a burden to him. Yes, he'd helped her through some serious rehabilitation on her leg and a sticky divorce with his asshole brother. And, yeah, he'd given her a place to live and a job. But he considered himself to be the lucky one.

"Come here." He crooked a finger at her, pulling her down on the sofa beside him. Swinging his arm around her shoulders, he tucked her in close.

"Holly, you know this is your house just as much as it is mine. You are welcome here anytime and you never, ever have to ask. Got me?" He kept his voice low, bordering on the edge of stern. He wanted her to realize how serious he was.

Holly shifted around so she could look up at him. "I know. It's just, well, things are different now that I'm married to Brax. I figured maybe I shouldn't just come and go as I please."

"Holly, you are and always will be my sister. Wherever I live is your home as well. No matter what is going on in either of our lives that will never change, understand?"

A smile crossed her lips, and she hugged him tight. "Thanks, Derrick."

"No thanks needed." He ran his finger down her cheek. "You're looking a bit pale, is everything all right with you? The drive isn't getting to be too much?"

She leaned back, rolling her eyes. "You're starting to sound like Brax. You know a lot of people have longer commutes than I do."

"Yes, but they aren't my sister," he said, watching her worriedly. She was pale. Too pale.

"What is this appointment you have tomorrow?"

It was the reason she and Brax were staying over the night. Derrick hadn't really questioned her about it, but from the way she couldn't meet his gaze, he now wondered if that had been a mistake. A surge of alarm filled him.

"Oh, it's nothing," she said with a dismissive wave of her hand.

"Holly," he said warningly, turning her to face him. "Spill."

She sighed. "Brax and I promised each other that we wouldn't tell anyone until we'd been to the doctor, but, well, we're pregnant!"

Derrick sat back in shock. He hadn't expected that. He stood, swooping Holly up in a big hug and swinging her around.

"Oh, love, that's fantastic." He set her on her feet. "I'm going to be an uncle."

"Well, we've only done a home pregnancy test, and although they're meant to be pretty accurate, I want to check with the doctor."

"You've got an appointment with an obstetrician tomorrow? Have you researched them? Do they have a good reputation?"

"Whoa." Holly held out her hands, laughing. "I've done my research. Dr. Francis has an excellent reputation; she's very popular, so we had to take the first available appointment."

"Good. Here, sit down. Bloody hell, I shouldn't be swinging you around like that. Are you feeling all right?"

"I'm fine. Just a bit tired. I haven't been sick yet, although I'm sure that's coming."

Derrick frowned. "How far along are you?"

"About 6 weeks."

"You shouldn't be traveling so much if you're pregnant, you need to get more rest."

She blew out a frustrated breath. "Derrick, please, I'm fine. I don't need both you and Brax on my case."

He knew when to back down. Although he would be talking to Brax about this the first chance he got. Holly needed to take things easier. It was probably time he started looking for another assistant. Maybe someone to help out part time so Holly could just work from home.

He'd miss her terribly, but her health came first.

"Okay then, love. Let's order that takeout. What's healthy for a pregnant woman to eat?"

IN THE END, they settled for pizza. Brax arrived a few minutes after the pizza was delivered. After finishing their meal, they all sat in the living room. Derrick leaned back on the sofa with a yawn.

"You look tired, man. Somethin' going on?" Brax asked.

Holly sat snuggled against Brax on the sofa. "He's been preoccupied for the last two weeks." She tapped her chin. "You're not having nightmares after that accident, are you?"

Derrick held back his smile. It was nice to have someone concerned about him. "No love. No nightmares."

"Then what is it? I'm worried about you."

Brax gave him a long stare, one that very clearly told Derrick he better clear this up right now and put Holly's mind at ease. Derrick nodded. In that, they were both in agreement.

Derrick sighed. "I've been thinking about the girl I met at the accident."

"Cece?" Holly asked her eyes widening.

"No." Like he'd want anything to do with that spoiled brat. Turned out she had been driving under the influence. She could very easily have hit Jacey or another car and killed someone. No, he hadn't wasted any time thinking about her.

Another reason why Jacey had no business out walking in the middle of the night. That was something he'd never allow if she were his.

"I've been thinking about Jacey, the other woman I met that night."

"Oh," Holly said, glancing up at Brax.

"I can't stop thinking about her. I wish I knew she was all right."

"Have you got any reason to suspect that she isn't okay?" Brax asked, with a frown. Brax was a Dom as well, and he knew all about the driving need to protect someone smaller and more vulnerable than himself.

"I don't know, just a feeling."

"Maybe you should try and find her. Do you know her last name?" Holly asked.

He shook his head. "And the only address I have for her is a large apartment building."

"Well, it's a start, isn't it?" Brax said. "And if you are thinking about her this much then you probably need to try and find her. For your peace of mind as much as anything else."

"I think I've found her."

Stephan Worthington sat up straight, gripping his phone tightly.

"What? Seriously?"

His stepbrother laughed. It was low, menacing sound. Stephan held back a shudder. Although Evan came in handy, particularly when Stephan had a job he didn't want to get his hands dirty with, he could never fully trust him. There was something wrong with Evan.

When they were young, pet rabbits and dogs started to go missing in their neighborhood. Stephan knew it had something to do with Evan, although his father had never suspected his stepson as the culprit. Evan's mother, Stephan's stepmother, might have known, but she would never accuse her precious son of doing anything wrong.

As they'd grown older, Stephan had found ways to use Evan's lack of a conscience to his advantage, but he always figured there would come a time when he would have to do something about Evan.

Something permanent.

"How did you find her?"

"It was easy. Stupid bitch got her picture in the paper. I've had my team on the lookout across the country. Two weeks ago, she was in a newspaper in Austin, Texas."

"What? Why was she in the news?"

She wouldn't dare go to the press about him, would she? She had to know that would be a death sentence.

"Oh, she was being a Good Samaritan. She happened to be one of the first people on the scene when that stupid bitch, Cece, had a car accident."

"Wait, you said that was two weeks ago, she could have moved on by now. What took your team so long?"

Stephan wasn't even sure who Evan's team was. Didn't want to know, quite frankly.

"It's a big country. We've had a lot of places to look." Evan's voice grew increasingly agitated. "And she didn't give them her name, so it didn't come up in any of our online searches."

"You're right, I'm sorry," Stephan soothed. "You did an excellent job. What now? Have you sent someone out there?"

What the hell was she doing in Texas?

"Since you're my brother, I'm going myself. Don't worry. I'll take care of that little problem."

~

"So, the doctor said everything is all right?" Derrick asked.

He stared over at a beaming Holly, who lay resting on a lounger by his outdoor pool.

"Yep, everything is great. We have to go back in six weeks for an ultrasound to check on the baby, and she gave us some information to read."

Brax was currently thumbing through a number of pamphlets. "There's a lot of information here. A lot of stuff you can't eat. No more coffee, either."

Derrick's eyes widened. "Seriously? How will you survive? Aren't you nine-tenths caffeine?"

"Smart ass." Holly whacked him on the arm. "And I can have one coffee a day."

Brax just grunted.

"I suppose we'd better go get ready then head back home," Holly said, standing.

"Not so fast. I bought something for you."

"What?"

"It's a gift."

"Derrick, you didn't have to do that," she protested.

"Yes, I did. I've wanted to do this for a while. Follow me." He led them through the house and into the attached garage, where a late model Volvo sat.

"You bought a new car?" Holly queried, looking puzzled.

"No, I bought you a new car. It has a top safety rating, traction control, airbags and I had a navigational system put in. That tin can you're driving isn't safe. I saw what can happen when a car like that is in an accident, and it's not pretty. With all this commuting and a baby on the way, I want you driving something safer."

"As do I," Brax agreed.

Holly turned to look at him. "You knew about this?"

He shrugged. "Derrick called me to ask what I thought. That's why I was a bit late getting here last night; I stopped to check the car over."

"And neither of you thought to ask me? I should get a say in this. I like the car I have."

"And just how are you going to get a car seat and stroller and everything else you'll need into the car you currently have, sweetheart?" Brax asked.

Holly bit her lower lip. "All right, point taken. But I have plenty of time to look for a new car."

"Now you don't have to," Derrick said. "I found you one of the safest cars available. Call it an early birthday present."

"My birthday is in November, Derrick." She turned to Brax. "You're really okay with this?"

Brax smiled. "Derrick can be very convincing, and he wanted to do this for you, and now for the baby as well."

"Holly, you're the only family I have. The only person I love. This car is the very least I can do to keep you safe."

Derrick knew he had won when Holly flung herself into his arms.

"Thank you, you over-protective, bossy, brother."

"You're welcome, my equally bossy sister."

5

Derrick ran his hand through his hair in frustration. He didn't understand why he was so determined to find her, he just knew he had to see her again. Only where did he start? Why hadn't he walked her to her door?

She'd insisted she'd be fine walking to her apartment on her own and he hadn't pushed her. He had understood her wariness, even applauded it. A woman alone couldn't be too careful. They didn't know each other, after all. And she shouldn't trust him with too much personal information.

But once she did know him then he would make it clear that she never had to fear him.

At least he knew where she lived. The building only had about 250 apartments.

Piece of cake, right?

He snorted. "Well, I'm not going to find her sitting here."

A small female stepped out of the apartment building, and he paused, heart racing. No, her hair was longer than Jacey's, darker. He watched as the woman walked down the block, entering a diner.

Why hadn't he thought of that? No doubt a lot of people around here frequented this diner. Hopefully, Jacey did as well.

He left his car and locked it before crossing the road and entered the diner.

He came to a standstill, shock holding him immobile as he spotted the waitress across the room. Her back was to him, but he'd still recognize her anywhere.

"Excuse me," someone said behind him.

"Sorry," he said, moving out of the way. Satisfaction filled him.

Damn, his luck was looking up.

EXHAUSTION FLOODED her as she struggled to concentrate on the order she was taking. She longed to sit with her feet up, sipping a glass of iced tea. She'd been working for close to ten hours, and she was exhausted. Not that she would ever complain.

More hours meant more money, and she needed every penny. One of the other waitresses had called in sick, and she'd snapped up the extra hours. She only had about twenty minutes of this shift left, she could get through it.

"Jacey."

She stilled. She recognised the voice. She should. The memory of his voice had been keeping her awake at night. "Jacey." His voice shivered down her spine as need flooded her, pooling between her legs, making her clit throb.

Wow. She had never reacted to Stephan like this. Slowly, she turned, hardly daring to believe her eyes.

Derrick smiled at her. "I was hoping I'd get to see you again."

She cleared her throat. "You were?"

He nodded. "Are you due for a break soon? Maybe you'll sit with me for a moment?"

What to do? She should turn him down. Things couldn't go any further between them. There were too many obstacles in their path. Of course, that was supposing he was even interested in her that way. Maybe he just wanted to talk about what happened the other night.

Disappointment filled her at the thought. There was something so irresistible about him. Like a whole container of Ben and Jerry's Chunky Monkey when she was on a diet.

Bad idea. Oh, but it would taste so good.

"I'm finished in twenty minutes. Can I get you something to eat or drink?"

"I'll take some iced tea."

Jacey nodded with a shaky smile, watching as he slipped into a booth. Shrugging off her surprise, she walked over to the kitchen and grabbing the jug of iced tea poured a large glass.

"Wow, that is one spunky hunk of a man sitting in your area, girl." Frankie stepped through the door into the kitchen, fanning herself. "If I was a few years younger, I'd be drooling all over him." Frankie had to be at least sixty.

Jacey smiled at her. "What are you talking about, if you were younger? You don't look a day over twenty-five."

"If only," Frankie replied with a laugh, waving her finger at Jacey.

Jacey picked up the glass of tea and carried it out to Derrick. Frankie was right, he was definitely a hunk with his dark hair and intense eyes.

The last part of her shift went by in a blur, and soon she was out the back, changing into her regular clothes.

Due to a high employee turnover, the diner's owner kept a few spare uniforms in the back. She wasn't sure how often he washed them, but she was grateful that she didn't have to wash it or transport it around.

She fingered the uniform as she hung it up. Things would be so much easier if she had a permanent job. But that would mean tax forms and social security numbers and Stephan on her doorstep. She had to be careful. He had the resources to find her.

Jacey grabbed her backpack out of one of the lockers then stepped back into the eating area of the diner. A wave of queasiness rushed over her, and she took a deep breath, putting a calming hand on her stomach. She needed to eat.

"Go sit down," Frankie called out to her. "I'll bring you a burger."

She smiled her thanks then made her way over to Derrick.

"Hi," she said as she stood beside his booth. Derrick quickly slid out and stood.

"Have a seat, love. Can I get you a drink or something?"

"It's okay. Frankie is bringing over something for me." She'd started her shift at six this morning and had only managed a few bites of a sandwich during her shift. Now she was shaking with hunger and fatigue. Frankie bustled over with a large burger and glass of iced tea. Jacey looked over at Derrick awkwardly. "Sorry, late lunch. Would you like something?"

She owed him for the pie the other night.

He shook his head and leaned back. "Please, go ahead."

She forced herself not to wolf the food down. Eating too fast when she had an empty stomach would only make her sick. She'd learned that the hard way.

Derrick was silent as she ate, but it wasn't an awkward silence. In fact, she was surprised by how at ease she felt around him.

"Come out to dinner with me," he finally said.

"Umm." She glanced down at her near-empty plate.

Derrick's lips twitched. "Maybe not tonight. Tomorrow night. I'll pick you up."

"Derrick, we don't even know each other."

"Which is why we need to go out to dinner. To get to know each other. I wasn't sure I'd find you so I couldn't believe my luck when I walked into this diner and saw you. I haven't been able to stop thinking about you. Jacey, I want to get to know you better."

She stared at him in surprise and disappointment. In another time and place, she would gladly have jumped on his offer. But she couldn't afford to get close to him. What if she trusted him and he ended up like Stephan? Obviously, her judgment when it came to men was crap.

Then there were all the secrets she was hiding. Even if he was as genuine as he appeared, she couldn't lump him with all her issues. That's assuming he didn't run for the hills once he heard the whole sordid tale.

"Ahh, Derrick—"

He held up his hand. "I can tell you're going to say no, so I want you to think about it. When's your next shift?"

"I'm working the breakfast shift every day this week." She was covering for one of the other waitresses. Shit. She probably shouldn't have told him that. He could still be a psychopath trying to lure her into his damp, dark basement. Her fatigue was making it hard to guard her words.

She needed to end this now before either of their feelings got involved. As she opened her mouth to speak, he stood.

"Good." He grinned. Pulling out his wallet, he grabbed some cash.

"That's too much," she protested.

"The service was excellent." Standing, he leaned down and kissed her on the cheek.

"I'll see you tomorrow."

Oh God, what was she getting herself into? She placed her hand on her cheek as it tingled.

Shaking herself out of her stupor, she picked up the cash he'd left, gaping at it in disbelief. Fifty dollars? The iced tea had cost $1.50.

Shaking her head, she placed the cash into her pocket, she'd give most of it back to him tomorrow.

A smile curved her lips. She was actually looking forward to seeing him again.

∽

A WEEK LATER, Jacey bit back a yawn as she walked toward the diner for her breakfast shift.

She just couldn't get used to sleeping in the shelter. It was too crowded and noisy, and she could never completely let down her guard. Add her poor sleep to these early morning shifts at the diner, plus the fatigue from being pregnant and Jacey felt like she was running on empty.

Didn't help that she'd cut her caffeine intake down drastically.

Oh, baby, the things I do for you. She patted her still flat belly with one hand, before slipping on her uniform. She didn't regret a single thing she had to do to keep her and her baby safe, including hiding from her abusive husband. She hadn't known she was pregnant when she'd run from Stephan, but she was extremely glad she'd left him before he found out. No way would her baby be raised by that bastard.

Pushing Stephan out of her mind, Jacey got to work.

Hours later, she stifled a yawn. There was another hour left of her shift, and Derrick had yet to show up today. She forced down the wave of disappointment. It was for the best. Derrick had been at the diner every day that week, trying to convince her to go out on a date with him. So far, she had managed to turn him down. But she was weakening under all that sexy charm.

She looked forward to seeing him each day. He always stayed for a while, cajoling her into taking her break with him. They would talk like they'd known each other for years. She felt like she already knew him better than she'd ever known Stephan. It was crazy, she would be better off chasing him away, not dancing around like a giggling teenager every time she thought of him.

It wasn't like she was ever going to take him up on his offer. She could never date him; there were just too many obstacles in her path. Too many lies, like where she lived and who she really was. Oh, and then there was the fact that she had a husband she was on the run from and was ten weeks pregnant with his child.

Yeah, not exactly something you can just blurt out over dessert.

She'd tried to give him back the fifty dollars he'd left the first day. He'd taken it, only the next time he'd left one hundred dollars instead. Finally, she'd had to tell him that she couldn't be bought. From the look of shock on his face, she'd realised that he hadn't been thinking about her that way, which had eased her indignation. He'd stopped leaving such huge tips, although they were still generous.

No, it was best if he gave up, no matter how much she enjoyed seeing him.

She placed a heaping plate of sausages, biscuits and fried eggs in front of one of the regulars before heading over to clean the table of a group that had just left.

Tucking the small tip into her apron, she cleaned up the mess they'd left. Balancing some plates on her arm, Jacey turned, coming to a stop with a gasp. The plates teetered on her arm. Large hands grasped the plates, before they ended up on the floor, taking them from her.

"Derrick, you scared me!"

He gave her a long, searching look. "Sorry, love. I did say your name, but you seemed to be deep in thought."

"Oh, right. Let me, umm, put these plates in the kitchen and I'll come back to take your order."

"Actually, I don't have time to eat. I just wanted to speak to you for a moment." He placed the dirty plates on the table and gestured for her to sit. Jacey glanced around; all of her customers seemed to be happy for the moment.

She sat.

Derrick reached across and took her hand, running his thumb over her knuckles. "I have to go away for a few days. I leave early tomorrow morning, and I'm not sure when I'll be back."

"Oh, well...ahh, have a good time." There was that disappointment again. She was getting far too attached to him.

His lips twitched. "It's business, love, not pleasure. Have dinner with me tonight, before I go."

The temptation was so great. She knew she shouldn't, but this might be the last time she saw him. She really should move on. Staying in one place too long probably wasn't a wise idea.

"I'm not sure..."

"Please, I'm begging." He widened his eyes and stuck out his lower lip. She giggled. Derrick wasn't a man who begged well. She figured he'd never had much practice.

"That's a pretty pathetic puppy dog face," she told him.

He placed his hand on his chest. "You wound me. I thought it was an excellent attempt. You're a hard woman. First, you reject me then you insult me. Do I need to beg?"

No, he didn't. If only her life was different. Less complicated. But it was what it was, and she had to do her best. Still, would one night matter? A night where she didn't have to think about anything else and could just have some fun. Where she could pretend to be normal.

"I don't have anything to wear."

"We'll go wherever you like. You choose."

Okay, maybe she could do this. She enjoyed being with him, and she was lonely. A night out could be what she needed.

"You know where Cece had her accident? Around the corner, there's a Thai place. I'll meet you out front." It was cheap, and she'd eaten there a couple of times when she couldn't get into the shelter for a meal.

"I'll pick you up." He frowned.

She shook her head. "I'll meet you, or it's no deal."

"Okay, love, you drive a hard bargain. Seven tonight it is." He kissed her cheek, his lips lingering.

6

Jacey stood on the street, waiting for Derrick. She knew she was early, but each minute she waited, doubt and nerves settled in.

She shifted from one foot to another. What had she been thinking, agreeing to this? She had no business going out for dinner with anyone at the moment. She needed to keep her head down and concentrate on herself and the baby.

But Derrick was hard to resist. She only hoped she wasn't making the same mistakes all over again.

When she had first met Stephan, there had been something about his take-charge attitude that had intrigued her. She'd thought him protective, caring, strong.

She had been so wrong.

Was she also wrong about Derrick? Could he be an asshole as well? Maybe all dominant men were? Maybe everything she had read about how protective and loving dominant men could be was really just fiction. Nerves bubbling, she turned to walk away. This was stupid.

"Jacey!" Derrick called out.

She stopped, unable to ignore the command in his voice. Damn it.

Turning, she watched Derrick stride toward her, her throat dry. She swallowed, trying to find her voice. He was so handsome, he took her breath away.

He stopped in front of her, holding out his hand. Against her better judgment, she let him take her hand in his. Tingles of pleasure raced up her arm, her nipples instantly hardening.

"You weren't leaving, were you?" he asked.

"N-no," she stuttered.

He stared down at her knowingly. She'd thought she was getting better at lying, but it seemed Derrick saw straight through her.

Then he smiled and letting go of her hand, held out his arm. She slipped her hand into the crook of his elbow.

"Good," he said. "I have been looking forward to this all day. I would hate to be deprived of your company."

"You'll probably be disappointed. I'm not that interesting."

"Hey. Look at me."

Jacey glanced up at him.

"You could never disappoint me."

Oh, if only he knew. But she gave him a small smile and straightened her shoulders. What was up with all this self-pity? Must be fatigue, she always grew more emotional whenever she was tired.

"Let's go eat. I'm starving." Derrick patted his stomach, and Jacey snorted, leading him to the restaurant. It didn't look like much from the outside, and she snuck a glance up at him.

Derrick's expression didn't change, though. He just reached forward and opened the door.

"Ladies first."

~

JACEY CHUCKLED as she and Derrick left the restaurant. She'd spent most of the evening laughing and eating. She felt pleasantly full and happy.

As she stepped out onto the pavement, reality hit her. Derrick wasn't hers. This was just a one-time thing.

And now she had to say goodbye.

"I had a really good night," she said, stopping so she could face him. Who knew he'd have such a good sense of humor?

"That sounds like you're saying goodbye," he murmured, cupping her cheek. "Let me drive you to your apartment. I'll walk you through the door, we can neck for a bit and then once we're all hot and bothered you can tell me goodbye."

"Neck?" She giggled. "Nobody says neck anymore. I'm pretty sure that went out in the fifties."

He shrugged good-naturedly. "I can be a bit old-fashioned."

"Have long have you lived in the states?"

She was changing the topic, but he didn't seem to mind.

"Nearly thirteen years, long enough for me to lose most of my accent."

"Do you miss your home?" she asked.

He looked off into the distance. "Sometimes." A sad look crossed his face.

Jacey tugged on his hand. "Take me home with you." It was incredibly bold. Something the old Jacey would never have done. But it was time to embrace the new her, the Jacey that had escaped her abusive husband, who was trying to carve out a life for her and her baby. She was more determined and stronger than she had ever thought.

She could have refused a ride home with him. Could have asked him to drop her off at the same place as the other night, but she was lonely. She wanted just one night where she felt safe and happy. Derrick could give her that. Maybe it was the sense of safety he exuded or the way he'd taken care of her all night, opening her door, pulling out her chair, making sure her food was all right and that she was warm enough, but right at that moment, she was willing to throw caution away.

She needed to move on, and after tonight she'd probably never see him again. She could have this one night. Something just for her.

His eyes widened as he stared down at her.

"Are you sure?" he asked.

She nodded. "I'm sure. Let's go." *Before I change my mind.*

Thankfully, he wrapped his arm around her waist and led her down the street to his car.

~

By the time, Derrick pulled up in front of his sprawling two-story home; he could tell that Jacey's nerves were starting to get the better of her. She'd grown increasingly pale, and her hands were clenched together on her lap. That backpack she carried with her everywhere was tightly pressed between her legs. One leg jiggled up and down as she looked nervously up at his house.

It didn't seem like she had much, her clothes were worn, her backpack scruffy and well-used. Would his house intimidate her? Glancing up at it, he wondered if he shouldn't have gone with something smaller. But he liked plenty of space and hated having neighbors pinning him in.

"Too much?" he asked.

Jacey turned to look at him. "What?"

Good, at least she was focused on him now.

"The house, is it too much? A bit gaudy?"

Her lips twitched. "Gaudy?"

"What? Another word that went out in the fifties?"

"No." She shook her head. "I think that one went out well before then."

"Cheeky brat," he told her with a grin. Reaching out he grabbed her hand. "Jacey, it's just a house. I promise that nothing is going to happen here that you don't want to happen. We can just go in and have a nightcap, maybe watch a movie. You can stay in the spare bedroom if you want or I can drive you home. It's entirely—"

"Derrick," she interrupted.

"Yes?"

"Shut up and kiss me." Leaning over, she grabbed his face between her hands and kissed him. He soon took over the kiss, thrusting his tongue between her lips. He drew her closer wanting to drink her in.

When he finally pulled back, they were both breathing deeply, and his cock was pressed against his pants, demanding release.

Jacey's cheeks were red, her eyes dazed.

"Wow."

"Yes," he agreed, trying to calm his racing heart. "Let's take this inside."

He kept a firm hold on her hand as he led her into his house as if he were afraid she might disappear.

"Do you have a basement?" she asked suddenly.

"A basement? No, why."

She smiled. "No reason." She paused in the foyer to remove her shoes.

"Don't worry about your shoes, love," he told her.

Shrugging, she pushed them to the side. "Does anyone else live here?"

He shook his head. "I have a housekeeper, but she lives offsite. Robert, my handyman, lives above the garage. Sometimes Holly stays, but not very often."

"So this whole house is for you?"

"Yep, house, grounds, pool."

"Oh... you have a pool."

He heard the longing in her voice. "Come," he commanded, pulling her through the large living area to the French doors that led out to the pool. He opened the doors and walked outside. She followed. Switching on the outdoor lights, he turned to face her.

Jacey's face filled with longing as she stared down at the pool. It was definitely warm enough for a swim.

"Let's go for a swim." He was already stripping off his shirt.

She shook her head. "I don't have a bathing suit."

"You have a bra and panties, same thing." And then she would have to stay here until they dried. He'd meant what he'd said. He was happy if she decided she wanted to just have a drink then sleep in the spare room. He wasn't interested in sex. Well, no, that was wrong. He was definitely interested in sex. But that wasn't the main reason he had brought her home with him. He wanted her to trust him. He wanted to know her better. He wanted to spend as much time as he could with her.

So yeah, he wanted to fuck her. Of course, he did. But this wasn't some one-night stand. He didn't bring just anyone back to his house.

They had to be special, and Jacey was definitely that.

She watched him, seemingly riveted as he stripped down to his underwear. He was gratified by the way her eyes widened, her breathing quickening as zeroed in on his erection pressing against his underwear. Derrick let her look for a long moment before turning and diving into the pool. Maybe the water would help cool his raging libido.

Then again, maybe not. He watched as Jacey stripped. Pulling off her pink shirt, she folded it neatly. She hesitated a moment then quickly stripped off her jeans.

Her bra was a plain white cotton, her panties green and lacy. Her pale skin gleamed under the lights.

My God, she's beautiful.

She crouched down, sitting on the side of the pool with her legs dangling in. Pale-skinned and slightly built, her breasts were small, her stomach slightly curved, her legs muscular—no doubt from being on her feet all day at the diner.

He frowned. She often looked pale and tired, and he worried she worked too hard. But tonight wasn't the night to discuss that.

"Come in. Or are you chicken?"

Wrinkling her nose at him, she pushed off, letting herself fully submerge in the water. Coming up, she pushed her dark hair back off her face, a huge grin forming.

"This feels so good."

Derrick dove beneath the water, and grabbing her, threw her into the air toward the middle of the pool. With a squeal, she landed with a splash and came up coughing.

"You rat! You're going to pay for that."

They played. Splashing each other. Jacey squealing as he chased her from one end to the other. Derrick hadn't felt so carefree in years. Finally, he grabbed hold of her, pulling her toward the shallow end of the pool. He pinned her between his body and the side of the pool. Capturing her wrists with one hand, he grinned.

"Got you now."

She wriggled playfully.

"Are you going to surrender?"

"Never!" she told him, with a wide grin.

"A dare." He used his free hand to tickle her under her arms.

"No, no, no," she squealed, laughing as she attempted to twist away.

"Do you surrender?"

"No!"

Leaning in, he kissed her deeply, cupping one of her breasts. It filled his palm nicely. He could feel her firm nipple through her thin bra.

"Do you surrender now?" he whispered.

"Yes."

"Good girl." He kissed his way down her neck to her shoulders, nipping the part where her shoulder and neck met. She leaned against him. He let go of her hands so he could run his hands down her sides.

"Put your legs around my waist," he told her, lifting her up. She slid her legs around him, her pussy against his waist. He nuzzled between her breasts, then reaching around, undid her bra, pulling it off and flinging it away to reveal her beautiful breasts. Leaning down, he sucked one nipple into his mouth while squeezing the other between his finger and thumb.

"Oh, oh," she cried out, pressing herself against him. Derrick slid his free hand down to cover her ass, squeezing the firm cheek as he continued to torture her breasts.

"Derrick, oh God."

"Like that, baby?" he asked.

"Umm-hmm," she replied, her head lolling back.

"Good. If you want to stop, tell me now," he whispered harshly.

His cock throbbed, protesting his words. But the last thing he wanted was to scare her away or overwhelm her.

"You stop now, and I'll hurt you," she said fiercely, surprising him. That slightly reserved air had disappeared throughout the night, revealing a passionate, rather feisty woman.

He liked it.

Her full breasts bobbed just above the water. He lifted her higher, nuzzling between her breasts before lapping at her right nipple.

Lick. Nibble. Suck.

Repeat.

Absolutely delicious. He moved across to her other nipple. Jacey twisted her fingers through his hair, not painfully, but enough to let him know how affected she was.

"You're so beautiful. I need to taste all of you." Desire swamped him, rushing over him in waves.

He lifted her, sitting her on the side of the pool, kissing her lower stomach.

"Lie back."

"Derrick..." she said hesitantly.

"Please," he forced out, holding back his natural need to command her. Jacey wasn't his sub; he wasn't sure how she would react if he were to completely take the reins.

She lay back.

"Tell me if you get cold," he told her, running his hand up her smooth, firm limbs. Reaching for her tiny panties, he tugged them off, revealing her pussy to his gaze.

He cupped her, loving the way she shuddered.

"I've been dreaming of this since I met you, Jacey."

"You have?"

"Oh yes."

He couldn't wait to taste her. Take her. Forcing himself to slow down, Derrick grabbed her ankles, pushing her legs up, placing her feet flat on the edge of the pool. This opened her up entirely to him.

"Derrick, I don't—"

"Shh, just let me play for a bit. If you don't like what I'm doing, then I'll stop." He kissed one thigh then the other. Parting her labia, he took a long lick.

"You're delicious."

"I am?" she asked with surprise.

He flicked her clit a few times. "Has no one ever told you that?"

She tensed.

"Jacey," he warned, he wasn't about to let her hide anything from him.

"No," she told him. "I was told I didn't taste very good down there."

He could hear the shame in her voice and silently cursed the person who had made her feel that way.

"They were wrong," he told her firmly. "I could do that to you all day and never get enough of your taste."

She relaxed a little, and he knew just how to push those memories from her head. Leaning in, he swept his tongue up and down her folds, before driving his tongue deep inside her pussy.

"Oh," she cried, thrusting her hips up against his mouth. He held her down as he drove his tongue in and out.

"Derrick!"

He moved up to her clit, sucking it into his mouth. Dropping one hand down, he pushed two fingers deep inside her. Flicking her clit with his tongue, he thrust his fingers in and out, delighting in her cries of passion.

She clenched around his fingers, her whole body shuddering. But she didn't come.

"Come for me, baby."

Jacey let out a low moan.

"Come now!"

With a scream, she came.

7

Jacey could scarcely believe that she'd just come, rather loudly, in Derrick's backyard. She'd been faking her orgasms with Stephan long before she'd left him and had fully thought she'd have to do the same tonight. Instead, she'd experienced a truly mind-blowing orgasm.

Derrick held her tighter as he climbed the stairs. Leaning down, he kissed her forehead.

"Okay, baby?"

She nodded, snuggling her face against his bare chest. He'd wrapped her up in a thick, fluffy towel before drying himself off. Then he'd swept her up in his arms and carried her inside. When they reached the staircase, he pushed open the large double doors and walked into the biggest bedroom she'd ever seen. A bed so huge it had to be custom-made was against the far wall with floor to ceiling windows flanking it.

Masculine furniture was artfully placed around the room. There was even an enormous fireplace.

"This is amazing."

Derrick glanced around. "Yes, I suppose it is." He walked across the room, stepping into a big bathroom. Setting her down, he leaned into a shower that could easily fit four people and turned the water on.

"I'd run a bath," he said as she glanced over at the sunken Jacuzzi bath, "but I can't wait that long to have you."

Her gaze shot back to him, or more specifically, to where his impressive erection pressed heavily against his wet boxers.

Jacey swallowed, moving toward him. "I'm sorry. I should have offered to help you with that."

She reached out a hand to touch him, shocked when he clasped her hand, holding it away.

"Much as I long to have you touch me, and believe me I truly appreciate the thought, I think I would come in about two seconds. When I come, I intend to be inside you."

"There's always round two."

His gaze lit up, the skin around his eyes crinkling as he grinned. "Oh yes, you can bet on that. However, I'm not as young as I used to be and this doesn't bounce back as quickly as it once did." He gestured at his erection.

"I find that hard to believe. All you have to do is issue a command, and it wouldn't dare remain limp."

Derrick chuckled then drew her against him, flinging away the towel.

"Flattery will get you everywhere," he murmured.

"Even here?" she replied, slipping her hand between them to wrap it around his hard cock.

Derrick groaned. Taking a step back, he turned her. "Into the shower with you," he growled.

Jacey stepped into the enormous shower, adjusting the spray to her liking.

Derrick moved in behind her, now completely naked. Jacey turned, taking him in. He had a body that simply would not quit. Wide shoulders, muscular chest, a firm six-pack and then there was his cock.

Firm, long, thick.

She hadn't had a lot of experience with men, but Stephan certainly couldn't live up to Derrick in more ways than one.

"Like what you see?" he asked, reaching over to grab some body wash.

Speechless, she nodded.

Derrick chuckled as he squirted some body wash onto his hand. Lathering it up, he rubbed it over her shoulders and down each arm.

"I can wash myself," she told him.

"I guessed that seeing as you don't smell," he teased. "But I want to wash you right now. Are you really going to deny me?"

He paused, looking down at her. It would take a stronger woman than her to deny him anything. Jacey shook her head, and he continued to soap her neck down to her breasts. Swirling the suds around them, he took great care to wash every inch, particularly her nipples which he massaged, lightly pinching until Jacey was swaying in pleasure, barely able to breathe.

Cupping them, he ran his thumbs over her nipples while staring down at her.

"Your breasts are very sensitive."

She nodded, even though it wasn't a question. "They're too small."

"Too small? I think not. They're perfect."

Derrick moved his hands down her stomach. She only had the slightest pouch there, nothing too noticeable, but she still tensed slightly as Derrick knelt and placed a kiss on her stomach. But he never said anything, just continued to wash her, parting her legs so he could clean her intimately.

Jacey blushed, her whole face on fire as he washed her very thoroughly.

When he finally stood, she felt as though she would explode at any moment, who knew a shower could be such a turn on?

As he finished, she reached for the body wash, squirting some onto the palm of her hand.

"My turn."

DERRICK BIT back his smile at Jacey's determined look. Opening out his arms, he spread himself wide.

"Do your worst, beautiful."

Oh hell, those were famous last words, he thought minutes later. Had he known she was hell bent on torturing him, he wouldn't have been so flippant. Her tiny hands moved over every inch of him, washing his arms, his chest, his nipples. Then she knelt at his feet, her face inches from his hard dick and he prayed that he wouldn't come right then and there.

She moved her way slowly up his legs, and Derrick bit down on his lip, every muscle in his body aching with the need to simply pick her up, slam her against the wall and drive his way inside her.

Then she grabbed his cock.

"Jacey," he protested.

"What?" she said with fake innocence. "I'm just washing you like you did me."

Cheeky little brat, when he got out of here, he was going to... well, he was going to take her hard and fast, then soft and slow, then hopefully hard and fast again. She knew she was torturing him and she loved every second if the smile on her face was any indication.

After she'd lathered up his cock, she rinsed it off, taking care to get rid of every last soap sud.

"Right, get your ass up here," he said, reaching down for her.

"Oh no, I don't think so," she murmured. Grasping the base of his cock, she took the head into her mouth, sucking him in.

Dear Lord. Derrick leaned back against the shower, his legs suddenly weak, knowing he'd lost this battle.

If she was his sub, he'd spank her ass bright red for this bit of disobedience.

But she's not my sub.

Could she be? He wondered how she'd take being placed over his knee. Well, he supposed there was one way to find out.

Later. Much later.

All thoughts swept from his mind as she lapped at the head of his dick, digging her little tongue into the slit. His balls tightened, a fiery need building, mounting, as she sucked his shaft into the silken sheath of her mouth.

Derrick resisted the urge to wrap his hands in her hair and take control. Instead, he closed his eyes and tried desperately to find some of the control he prided himself on.

"Hell's bells," he muttered as she pumped the base of his cock with her hand in time with the sucking of her mouth. "I'm going to come, beautiful. If you want to pull back, do it now."

Jacey tightened her hold, upping her speed and Derrick let himself loose. He came in her mouth in large spurts, his whole body shaking as he lost himself in the pleasure of her touch.

JACEY LET Derrick finish rinsing them both off before he turned off the shower and stepped out. He grabbed a towel, holding it out for her. Stepping out, she reached for the towel, but he brushed away her hands away.

"Let me," he said gruffly, drying her thoroughly.

He wrapped a fresh towel around her then quickly dried himself off. Jacey couldn't help but stare at his luscious body. Incredibly, her pussy throbbed incessantly, wanting more.

Derrick took her hand, leading her into the bedroom, but instead of taking her straight to the bed, he steered her over to the sofa which faced the fireplace. Switching on the gas fireplace, he sat on the sofa then drew her down against him.

"How are you feeling, beautiful?"

"Umm, I'm okay." She wasn't quite expecting a heart to heart. She'd figured he would take her straight to bed.

Derrick chuckled and lifted her onto his lap. He arranged her legs, so she straddled his lap, facing. He pulled away the towel, throwing it on the floor.

"Let's try this again, shall we?" he murmured, flicking his finger over her nipple until it was taut and aching. "Tell me what you're feeling right now."

"Do we have to talk? Can't we just...you know?"

"Can't we just what?" he asked, the skin around his eyes crinkling. Bastard. He knew what she meant. "Can't we just get a midnight snack? Watch some TV? Snuggle in front of the fire?"

"Snuggle?" She bit her lip to stop herself from laughing. Derrick certainly didn't look like the type of man who would snuggle. He winked at her.

"You know what I meant," she said. "Can't we just go to bed?"

"You're tired?" He slipped his hand down her stomach to her pussy. She widened her legs without a thought, and he slid his fingers through her slick folds. "Do you want to go to sleep?"

"No," she groaned, thrusting her hips against his hand.

"What do you want?"

"More."

"More what?" he questioned.

"Why are you making me do this? Why are you making me talk? Can't we just have sex?"

His fingers stilled, and she whimpered.

"We could just fuck. But I want to know you, Jacey. I feel something for you, don't you feel it too?"

She should lie. Tell him this was just about the sex. But she'd never been a good liar, and he deserved at least some truth from her.

"Yes," she replied. "But I don't want to talk. There are things in my life that I can't talk about. All I can give you is tonight."

His eyes gleamed with determination. "We'll see," he whispered before taking her mouth with his, stalling any more protests. He swirled his fingers around her clit before flicking it, his movements increasing in speed until she was gasping with the need to come.

"So damn beautiful," he whispered. "I could watch you like this all day."

At that moment she came, bucking in his arms as he slowed his movements, drawing out her orgasm. She shuddered in his arms as he moved his fingers away from her pussy, sucking them into his mouth.

"So sweet."

Jacey ducked her head against his chest.

"Shy?" He tipped her chin up, meeting her gaze, his eyes like molten pools. "Jacey, I—"

Jacey slipped from his lap, kneeling on the floor between his legs. She drew his towel open to reveal the thick cock she'd felt pressing against her. She didn't want to talk. Talking couldn't lead anywhere good. Tonight, she just wanted to feel alive, to feel safe and wanted.

Because she knew there couldn't be a tomorrow for them.

She grasped hold of his firm cock, squeezing it lightly.

"On no, you don't, brat. Not again." Reaching out, he pulled her hand from his cock.

"You don't like it?" she asked.

Derrick raised a brow. "I think how quickly I came in your mouth earlier proves just how much I like you touching me. However, I already owe you a spanking for that little episode, do you really want to double it?"

Jacey quickly scooted back onto her butt, looking at him warily. Had he really just said that? Where was the caring guy from a few minutes ago? Had she messed up again? When the hell would she learn that her instincts, when it came to men, were shit?

"Whoa, Jacey, what's wrong? Did I scare you? I didn't mean to." Derrick held out his hand, and she shied back, holding her arm up to shield herself.

"Jacey," he whispered in shock. "Did you think I was going to hit you?"

"You just said you were!" She dropped her arm, feeling slightly embarrassed as his hand stayed where it was, held out to her. She stood up, feeling at a disadvantage with him looming over her.

"No, I said I was going to spank you. I would never harm you."

"You think a spanking doesn't hurt?" The beatings Stephan had laid out on her ass had left her in bed for days.

"Some do," Derrick admitted. "But I wasn't talking about a serious spanking. I'm sorry if I gave you that impression. I was talking about the sexy kind of spanking."

Sexy kind? What the hell did he mean?

"Spankings aren't sexy. Not for me."

Why was she standing here talking to him about this? Why wasn't she running as fast as she could?

Because something about him pulled at her. She wanted to trust him.

Because she didn't want this night to be over. She wasn't ready to be alone again.

"God, you're a Dom," she interrupted, disgusted with herself. "How did I not see that?"

Boy, did she know how to pick 'em. She'd sworn to never get involved with another Dom again, and here she was standing naked in front of him. He'd made her come twice. She'd gone down on him. Jacey covered her breasts with one arm, trying to shield her nakedness.

Did she have a sign on her face? Was it a scent she gave off? Or was she just attracted to assholes who liked to beat on people?

She knew that last thought wasn't fair, Derrick had done nothing to hurt her, but the abuse she'd experienced at Stephan's hands was still fresh in her mind.

"I can't do this," she whispered. In fairness, there had been signs. Derrick was definitely a man who liked to take charge. She'd just ignored what had been obvious because she'd liked him.

Stupid. Stupid.

Derrick held out his hand. "Jacey, wait, talk to me. Obviously, you know something about BDSM—"

"Enough to know I want nothing to do with it," she snapped back, looking around for her clothes. Where were they? Oh crap, they were still outside!

"Jacey, stop," Derrick commanded. She froze on her way to the door. "Look at me."

Move!

But her limbs wouldn't cooperate. She froze but refused to turn and face him.

"Okay, that will do. I obviously hit a trigger. Well, I think I bulldozed right on over it. I'm sorry for frightening you, and I want you to know that I would never harm you. You must trust me on some level to come home with me tonight, to let me touch you."

He was right. Crap.

"That's all changed now."

"Has it? I'm guessing you've had a bad experience with a Dom, but that wasn't me. Not all Doms are assholes. Doms have feelings too you know." The faint teasing in his voice had her turning to face him. She wished like hell she had some clothing on. But he was naked as well. Except Derrick embraced his nakedness with an ease she envied.

"You want to control me, punish me."

"I want to make you feel good. Control doesn't have to be a bad thing. Control doesn't mean abuse. I can be in control and still cherish you. Hell, this wasn't the conversation I thought I'd be having tonight." He ran his hand through his hair. "Jacey, you may not believe me, but I didn't bring you here with any ulterior motive or to play any sort of games. I just wanted us to be Derrick and Jacey. To get to know each other."

"You threatened to spank me."

"All in the name of fun."

There he went again. What fun? Fun for him, maybe. Not for her.

"And if I didn't want that? What then?"

"Then all you have to say is no."

"Men don't like to hear the word no."

"There you go again. I'm not him, Jacey. Although one day I hope you'll tell me exactly what he did to hurt you. I insist that you tell me if I ever make you uncomfortable, or frighten you. Why don't we come up with a safe word?"

Jacey took a step back. "I'm not a submissive, and I'm not doing any of that stuff again."

"I understand. You have my word I will not push or force you into anything you don't want. The safe word will just be about giving you control. I don't know all your triggers yet, just like you don't know mine."

"As long as you honor it."

His face hardened. "I will. I swear. I have never broken my word nor have I ever ignored a safe word."

"You've been doing this a long time?"

"Many, many years."

"So we'll both have a safe word then?"

Derrick raised a brow. "If you wish. What would you like yours to be?"

"Pink."

"Fair enough. Mine can be blue then."

Jacey rolled her eyes but relaxed slightly.

"Will you sit with me?" He held out his hand to her.

Probably a bad idea. But her feet were moving even as she thought that. She reached out and took his hand.

Derrick sighed as he sat on the sofa. She sat next to him, not quite touching him.

"Thank you."

"For what?" she asked.

"Trusting me, I know it can't be easy."

"You don't know how hard it is. And my trust only goes so far," she warned him.

He brushed her hair back off her face. "That's as it should be. I wouldn't want you trusting too easily. There are a lot of bad things in this world, and you should always be on alert."

There was a sad look in his eyes, as though he had first-hand experience. That was something she could relate to.

"I know. People you think you know can turn out to be total strangers."

Although it wasn't cold, Derrick pulled a blanket off the back of the sofa. Lying on his back, he tugged her down next to him. Jacey lay on her side, her head nested on his chest as he tucked the blanket around them both.

"Who hurt you?" His voice was quiet, undemanding, his heartbeat steady against her ear. Jacey yawned, feeling warm and safe with him. It seemed crazy when just minutes ago she was ready to flee.

"My ex."

Derrick ran his hand up and down her back.

"He turned into someone I didn't know, someone who seemed to hate me even as he said he loved me."

"How did you meet him?"

"Through my parents, they set me up with him. They thought he was wonderful, of course. So did I, in the beginning. I was taken in by his charm and his good looks. He was smart, rich, successful, well-liked and I thought I had found the man of my dreams."

"When did you learn differently?"

"After about ten months. Oh, there were little signs before then, things I foolishly ignored. I was so excited when he first told me he was a Dom." She snorted. "I had all these silly fantasies about what being with a Dom would be like, that he would be protective and caring, that he would put my needs and wants ahead of his own. That I would be able to surrender myself and trust him to look after me."

"What did he do instead?"

"He hurt me. What I saw as protectiveness turned into a blind, raging jealousy."

"He hurt you?"

She shook her head. "I can't." Part of her longed to confide in him, to let go of some of the burden, but she wasn't ready to trust him that much, to open herself up. "I can't talk about this." Her breath hitched, and she bit her lip, holding in her sob.

"Shh." He turned her head, kissing her softly on the lips. "It's okay. I'm not going to push you." She heard the silent, *for now*. But it didn't matter. She didn't plan on this happening again. This was a one-time thing, no matter her feelings for him.

He ran his finger across her lip, along her jaw, and down her neck.

"Derrick," she said, her breath coming faster.

He pulled his hand away, resting it on her thigh. The last thing he wanted to do was push her, risk her running from him. "Shall we go to bed, beautiful?"

She nodded her gaze wide as she stared down at his thick erection. "Oh yes."

Scooping her up into his arms, he carried her to his bed.

Derrick thrived on being in control, but he would tone that side of himself down until he'd gained her trust. When she was more comfortable, he'd ease her into his dominance in the bedroom gradually, over time. Because there was no way things were ending after tonight.

Derrick placed her on the bed, lying next to her on his side. Leaning in, he kissed her, taking her mouth fully, plunging his tongue inside. Jacey ran her fingernails softly over his chest, rubbing his nipples.

Scooting further down, he pressed her breasts together so he could lick both of her nipples at once. The hard nubs deepened in color as he played with them. He reached down and flicked at her clit before driving two fingers deep inside her, her juices easing his way. In and out.

Derrick stilled, nearly shouting out in surprise as she reached down and circled his dick, pumping him. He shuddered, his balls tightening as she played with him.

"Jacey, I'm not going to last if you do that," he warned.

"Neither am I if you keep playing with me."

"You don't need any recovery time."

"I want to come with you inside me, Derrick. Please."

Christ, like he could say no. Rolling over, he reached out to pull open the bedside table. Grabbing a condom, he quickly fitted it over himself.

Cupping her cheek, he looked into her eyes. "You're sure?"

She cupped his cheek, mimicking him. "Derrick, if you're not inside me in the next thirty seconds, I may explode."

Placing a scorching kiss on her lips, Derrick maneuvered himself between her legs. Grabbing her under each knee, he pushed her legs against her chest. Jacey grasped hold of her legs as he guided his cock into her entrance.

"Oh dear Lord, this is what heaven feels like," he groaned. "Fuck, so tight and hot."

He thrust fully inside her, both of them panting as though they had run a marathon. Jacey let her legs drop, her feet planting themselves on the mattress as she reached up and placed her hands around his neck.

Derrick pulled out then quickly drove back inside her. He clenched his teeth, felt the sweat pooling on his body, mingling with her own as he fucked her with slow, steady thrusts.

Jacey drove her hips up against him, and Derrick was lost. Letting himself go, he picked up the pace. With one hand he reached down to flick her clit.

"Soon, baby. Very soon. Get ready to come."

He felt her ripple around him, knew she was there.

"Come now." Two more thrusts and he came. He filled the condom in huge bursts, his body trembling with his release. Jacey cried out beneath him, pulsating around his cock, making him shudder with pleasure as she came.

Collapsing with exhaustion, he had the presence of mind to roll off her, drawing her into his side.

"Wow," she said.

He nodded, unable to speak, but in total agreement. Wow.

8

Jacey woke in the early hours of the morning. She blinked steadily for a moment, wondering where she was. It was too quiet for the shelter, and the bed was way more comfortable. She felt more relaxed and rested than she had in ages.

A soft snore drew her attention, and she rolled over to see Derrick lying on his back, his arm flung over his head, the sheet resting on his stomach.

She'd slept with him. What had she been thinking?

She'd been thinking that here was the sexiest man she'd ever met and he wanted her. Her. She'd been thinking it was a dream come true, one she couldn't pass up.

A one-night stand that she would remember for the rest of her life. She was going to be sore when she got up. Worth it, though. She grinned. Yeah, the sex had been amazing, but it was Derrick that had truly made it wonderful. He'd been nothing but kind and considerate, even when she'd freaked out on him.

But she couldn't forget that this was one night. As hard as it was going to be to leave, she had to. She had to separate herself from him.

For her own good.

Sitting carefully, she wondered if she could manage to climb out of bed and get in a shower without him waking up. Scooting over to the side of the bed, she swung her legs over the edge, screaming in surprise when a tanned, muscular arm surrounded her waist, dragging her back down.

"Just where to do you think you're going?" Derrick murmured in her ear.

"I have to get up for work," she told him. Already her body was reacting. Her clit throbbing as her nipples hardened.

"Surely we've got some time... ahh, damn, maybe not. I have a flight to catch this morning."

Twisting her around, he hugged her tight, kissing her deeply. "Hmm, I should have set my alarm for earlier."

"But you have to go and so do I." Truthfully, she wanted nothing more than to stay in bed with him. It was probably a good thing he was going away, give them both breathing space and stopping her from falling back into his arms and begging him to take her.

"You're right." He gazed down at her. "Take a shower in here, while I grab one in the guest bathroom. Do you have a change of clothes in your backpack?"

"Yes."

"Good. After we shower, I'll rustle up something for breakfast. Hopefully, you like omelettes. It's about all I can do."

"That's fine." Much better than the dry crackers she had in her backpack. Luckily, other than a bit of nausea, she hadn't suffered much morning sickness.

She showered quickly, changing into an old pair of jeans and a t-shirt. Combing her hair, she looked at herself in the mirror, studying the woman looking back at her. She looked thinner, tired, but this woman also looked like she'd been well-loved.

"Jacey, come down when you're ready," Derrick called out. "I'm going to get our clothes from outside and then start breakfast."

"Okay, thanks."

She gazed around the magnificent bedroom one more time,

drawing it into her memories. Last night was something she would remember forever.

※

Derrick pulled up outside the diner. "I want your phone number."

She shouldn't give it to him. She needed to end this now.

"Jacey, give me your number."

"Fine." She rattled it off, and he entered it into his phone. Just because he had her number didn't mean he would call. Or that she would answer.

Ahh, who was she kidding? Of course, she would answer.

He pulled her close and kissed her deeply.

"I better go," she said reluctantly.

He looked at the clock on his dashboard. "Me too. Take care."

"You too." She watched as he pulled away before striding around the building to the alley behind.

She walked up to the back door. Derrick had dropped her off outside the front of the diner, and she'd waved to him as he drove off, her lips still tingling from his kiss. He'd said he would see her when he got back, but she knew that was just talk. She'd probably never see him again.

For the best, she told herself, wishing she could believe it.

She was a bit early for work, but she knew Frankie would already be there. Frankie always arrived early. Sometimes she wondered if the other woman slept there.

Jacey knocked on the back door and waited for Frankie to open it. She shifted her backpack from one shoulder to the other.

The solid door opened but instead of seeing Frankie's smiling face, Jimmy stood there.

"Hi, Jimmy, how are you?" she greeted the owner of the diner.

The dour-looking man stared down at her. "Jacey, you're here."

Wasn't he expecting her?

"Umm, I'm working the breakfast shift to cover Wendy."

Jimmy shook his head, and her stomach took a nosedive. "Wendy's back."

"Oh, right. You'll text me about any other shifts?" She'd bought a prepaid phone, so he could get in touch with her. Only Jimmy and now Derrick had the number.

She tried to hide her disappointment about the lost money as she looked up at Jimmy. A look of guilt crossed his face, and her stomach gurgled in worry.

"Look, Jacey, you're a real good waitress, but my niece just moved to town, and she's looking for some part time work. Times are tough, and I can't employ you all. Family has to come first. You know how it is."

Sure, she knew. She was the easiest one to let go since she didn't really exist.

"Probably best if you start looking for work elsewhere."

"I understand, thanks for everything."

Thanks for everything? Thanks for what? Thanks for treating me like dirt when I worked my ass off for you? The words remained trapped inside, buried deep. Just like they always did.

Jacey turned away in a daze. What the hell was she going to do now? She didn't have near enough money saved for when the baby came. She couldn't sign up for any government assistance programs because of all the paperwork she'd have to fill out. That would be a target on her back that Stephan couldn't miss.

She bit her lip to hold in her sobs.

"Jacey! Jacey, wait up!" She turned to find Frankie running toward her.

The other woman stopped when she got close. "Jeez, girl, you're gonna give me a heart attack," she said, running her hand back and forth in front of her face. "How can you walk so fast with those short legs?"

"Jimmy let me go," Jacey said in a daze.

Frankie scowled. "I know. I hope you gave him an earful. That bastard."

Jacey shrugged. "He needed the work for his niece."

"His niece is a fat, lazy slob with the attention span of a two-year-old. Jimmy needs his head examined, and you should have told him off for treating you like dirt. Manners are well and good, sweetheart, but sometimes you just got to let it rip. Otherwise, your insides will get eaten away at with all the stress."

Jacey nodded. She was right. It wasn't anything Cady hadn't been trying to teach her. To speak her mind. To stand up for herself.

"Here, this is for you." Frankie handed her an envelope.

Jacey took it. "What's this?" She opened it up, her jaw dropping. Quickly, she thrust it back at Frankie. "I can't take this."

"Sure you can. It's my tips for the week, and I want you to have them."

"Frankie, no, you need this."

Frankie cupped her cheeks. "Not as much as you do, honey. Now, you come back and let me know that you're doing okay. Promise."

Tears filled her eyes at the older woman's kindness. "I promise."

~

DERRICK CLIMBED into the backseat of his town car after greeting Robert. Exhaustion washed over him. He'd been away five days, but it felt like a month. He was growing old. He hadn't slept well, either, which didn't help. He'd told himself it was because of the unknown surroundings. However he was a seasoned traveller and had never once been homesick.

No, the real reason he'd had trouble sleeping was because he'd been plagued with dreams about Jacey. Her touch, her smell, the little noises she made when she came. Getting any work done had been nearly impossible. And in the evenings she would sneak into his head, tormenting him.

He'd tried the number she'd given him, but there had been no answer. He'd spent endless hours wondering if she was okay. If she was safe. The area she lived in wasn't that bad, but she'd have been a lot safer in his house. Robert could have driven her to and from work and Derrick could have called her each night.

He glanced at his watch. It was early, she'd still be working her shift at the diner.

"Robert, change of plans. I feel like having breakfast." He gave his driver directions to the diner. Not like he was going to get any sleep until he'd seen her anyway.

9

"What do you mean she's not here?" Derrick asked with a frown. "Is it her day off?"

The overweight waitress, who couldn't be older than eighteen or nineteen, smacked some gum as she stared at him in boredom. She looked him up and down as though assessing him. Suddenly, she straightened.

"She got fired," the girl said. Chew, smack. Chew, smack. She reached out a hand, touching his chest. "But if you're looking for a good time, I can help ya."

Derrick barely held in a shudder of disgust. Fired? From what he'd observed, Jacey was a well-liked, efficient waitress.

Wasn't the end of the world, though. He didn't particularly like her being on her feet all day.

But he was sure she was devastated. And scared. He needed to find her.

"Can you give me her address?" It was probably against the rules, but he figured this kid was too dumb to know that.

"Her address?" she said slowly, reconfirming his view on her intelligence.

"Yes, I'm a friend. I know she lives in one of the apartments a few doors down, I just can't remember which one," he lied.

The girl let out a snort then started laughing. "Dude, don't know what sort of *'friend'* you are, but that Jacey didn't live in no apartment. She's homeless, man. That's why my uncle could let her go, 'cause she was off the books."

Derrick gaped at her. Homeless? No, that wasn't right. He would know if she was homeless. There was no way that he had left the diner every day to go home to his nice, warm house while she went to a shelter or worse, slept outside. There was no way that he had dropped her off here the other morning while she had nowhere to go.

"Sit down before you fall down." The older woman he'd seen a few times stood in front of him. She gave him a prod, and he sat on the seat behind him. "Go get some work done, you idiot," she barked at the girl.

The other waitress glared at her. "Shut up, old woman. My uncle owns this joint."

"Your uncle would kick your ass to the curb long before he'd think about firing me, girl. Go find something to do." The waitress smacked her gum as she turned away with a huff. "Stupid girl." Then she looked at him, her gaze shrewd.

"You want some coffee? You're looking pretty pale."

"No thanks, ma'am," he said politely, his mind still reeling.

"Please, don't call me ma'am, it makes me feel old. Frankie's my name."

"Was she lying?" he demanded.

Frankie sighed and shook her head, her tight curls barely bouncing with the movement. "I wish I could say the little cow was spreading lies, but unfortunately it's true."

"She's homeless," he whispered. "Why didn't she tell me? I could have helped her."

"Jacey is a proud woman. She was working to make a better life for herself. Well, she was until that little cow talked her uncle into hiring her." She gestured over toward where the young waitress was currently flirting with an overweight man in a suit that was bursting at the seams.

"I have to find her." Determination filled him. No way was she spending another night on the streets.

Frankie nodded, a look of relief entering her eyes. "Good. Jacey needs someone like you on her side."

"Any idea where I should start?"

Frankie nodded. "I'll write down the address of the shelter I think she uses most. It's not far from here. But she won't be there until tonight, and if she's not there, well, I'm not sure."

Derrick let out a deep breath, not sure how he was going to manage to wait until tonight, and if she wasn't there...

His stomach bubbled, making him feel ill. He would find her. He had to. He wasn't sure his sanity could survive the night thinking about her out there, alone and unprotected.

∽

"Look, you have to tell me if you've seen her. Is she here?" Derrick said with frustration.

The woman behind the counter eyed him suspiciously. "Actually, sir, I don't have to tell you anything. I think it might be best if you left."

Derrick ran his hand through his hair. He had never felt so desperate or so out of control of a situation in his life.

"I just want to help her, I'm a friend. Her name is Jacey, she's about five foot two with dark, curly hair and brown eyes. I have it on good authority that she stays here often, you must have seen her."

Derrick could hear his voice rising with agitation, but couldn't calm himself. Someone here knew her, and he wasn't giving up until he found her.

"Sir, I am not at liberty to share anything about the people who use this shelter. If she's such a good friend, I'm sure she will be in contact. Now, please leave."

"All right, how much is this going to cost me?" He pulled out his wallet and withdrew a couple of hundred dollar bills.

Her gaze went frosty. "Leave, now. Before I call the police."

Knowing he was now doing more harm than good, Derrick turned and walked out of the shelter.

Frustration and fear grew. What was he going to do now?

After leaving the diner, he'd driven over to the shelter to find it closed until evening. He'd then headed home to shower and change. Unable to sleep or eat. Instead, he'd researched on homeless shelters in the city, something that, to his shame, he'd never really paid much attention to.

But it was a very real problem. And his Jacey, his sweet, delicate Jacey was one of the homeless. He just couldn't believe it. Finally, unable to sit still any longer, he'd gotten into his car and driven around the streets of Austin until the shelter opened.

Part of him had still hoped that it was all a misunderstanding. That she worked there during the evenings and that's why Frankie had seen her walk into the place.

But he knew he was grasping at straws.

Moving toward his car, he opened the door, wondering what to do next.

"Hey, you!"

Derrick ignored the voice yelling out.

"Are you looking for Jacey or not?"

Derrick froze then turned, shutting his car door. A greasy-looking guy wearing a hoodie and track pants stood on the pavement, looking at him with calculating eyes. His long hair was pulled back in a ponytail. He could do with a shave and a shower. Or two.

"What did you say?" Derrick asked.

"My name's Ronald. I heard you tell that bitch inside that you was lookin' for Jacey. She stays here a lot."

"Do you know where she is now?" Derrick asked urgently.

The other man shook his head. "Haven't seen her. But I could let you know when she is here. For a price, of course."

Of course. Not that Derrick cared.

He nodded. "Hundred dollars if you call me as soon as you see her."

The guy snorted and shook his head. "Hundred bucks upfront. Five hundred when I call you."

"All right." Derrick grabbed his wallet and drew out a hundred dollar bill. "Give me your cell, and I'll put my number in." This could all be a trick, but right now he didn't care. He was desperate enough to try anything.

The man snorted. "Do I look like I carry around a cell phone?"

Derrick narrowed his gaze. "Just how were you going to call me?"

"I'll use the phone in there." The man nodded his greasy head toward the shelter.

"Not good enough. I'll get you a phone. Meet me back here in an hour."

After buying a cheap throwaway cell phone, he returned to meet up with Ronald. Then Derrick spent most of the night driving around the streets, looking for Jacey. By two a.m. his vision was blurring. He knew he had to go home and get some sleep before he became a hazard on the road. He tried calling her again. No answer.

Bloody hell, where was she?

∼

JACEY SHIVERED beneath the thin blanket covering her. It wasn't that cold, yet she couldn't stop shaking. *Please, don't let me be getting sick. Please.*

She really couldn't afford to get sick. She swallowed, her throat aching. Jacey rolled over on the small cot. She'd chosen a different shelter tonight, needing to get away from Ronald and his unwanted attention. But although she had protection from the elements, it just didn't seem to be enough to shake off this chill she'd developed.

She coughed into the pillow, hoping not to wake anyone around her. The cough was rough and crackly, and she sniffed as she felt her nose run. Not good. Jacey had spent the last two days searching for a job. Perhaps she'd overdone things, but she was desperate. She didn't have nearly enough money saved. And she needed every dime for the baby.

Her stomach cramped, stress making her feel ill. She had no choice but to get up in the morning and start searching again. With a sigh, Jacey tried to relax, knowing she needed sleep.

A vision of Derrick entered her mind. She wondered if he was back from his trip yet. Had he been thinking about her? She hadn't been able to get him out of her mind. The feel of his arms around her, how safe he made her feel, how easily he turned her on.

Jacey shook, only this time it had nothing to do with feeling ill, no the heat rushing through her blood was due to the memory of Derrick's mouth on her pussy, licking her clit.

It was going to be a long, long night.

∼

DERRICK GLANCED down at his phone as it buzzed. As soon as he saw the number on the screen, he jumped to his feet, not caring that he was in the middle of a meeting.

"I have to take this, excuse me," he managed to say as he walked swiftly out of the double doors.

"Ronald, you've seen her?"

"Yeah, just caught sight of her on Lavaca between 5th and 6th."

"Follow her," Derrick said urgently. "I'm on my way."

"That'll cost you extra," Ronald replied.

"I don't care. Just don't lose her." Derrick hung up and ran out of the building, sliding his cell phone into his pants pocket.

He pulled up to the curb and saw Ronald leaning against a crosswalk sign.

"Where is she?" Derrick asked as he climbed out of the car.

"About a block ahead of us," Ronald said.

Derrick started to take off when the other man grabbed his arm.

"Hey, where's my money?"

With a mutter of impatience, Derrick grabbed his wallet from his pocket and thrust some bills toward the other man, not looking back as he raced down the block, his heart pounding.

He came to a standstill as he saw her. She was walking slowly along the sidewalk.

Thank God.

Relief almost brought him to his knees.

Then he noticed how she weaved. She fell to one knee. His stomach dropped as he raced toward her. Had she tripped? Was she hurt?

"Jacey! Jacey?" He knelt beside her on the hard pavement, ignoring the people around him as he clasped her cheeks between his hands to raise her face. Shit, she was burning up.

"Oh hell, you're sick." Standing, he scooped her up into his arms. Turning, he carried her toward his car.

"Derrick?" she murmured. "What's going on?"

"Shh, baby. Just relax, I'm going to take care of you." He let her legs drift down as he reached into his pocket for his keys and unlocked his car. Opening the passenger door, he placed her inside.

"Derrick, this isn't a good idea," she said tiredly, opening her eyes to stare up at him as he buckled her in.

He brushed her hair off her face, worried about how pale she was.

"What's not a good idea is you wandering the streets when you're burning up with fever."

"I'm fine. It's just a cold." A cough wracked her body, and he winced at the wheezing sound as she gasped for breath. Leaning her forward, he rubbed her back.

"Come on, baby. Breathe, just breathe for me. Good girl. Now you just sit back and rest while I get you to the hospital."

He shut her door and ran around to the driver's side.

"Hospital?" she murmured. "No hospital...can't afford it."

"Don't you worry about it. I'll take care of it. Just like I'm going to take care of you."

Reaching over with one hand, he squeezed her thigh gently.

Despite the fact that he was worried about her health, a surge of relief and satisfaction filled him. He intended that nothing would happen to her again.

~

DERRICK WATCHED as the doctor examined Jacey. The nurse had already taken her vitals and changed her into a hideous hospital gown. He'd lied and told them he was her fiancé. Although they'd given her ringless finger a glance, they hadn't questioned him.

People normally didn't.

"Well?" he asked impatiently as the doctor stood back, pulling his stethoscope away from Jacey's back. The nurse helped Jacey lie back on the bed.

"Sounds like bronchitis, but we'll need to get an x-ray to rule out pneumonia."

"No…no x-ray," Jacey said quietly, opening her eyes.

"Jacey, it's okay." Derrick grabbed her hand, wanting to reassure her.

"No x-ray, it's not safe for the baby."

The doctor looked up from where he was writing on a clipboard.

"You're pregnant?" He looked to Derrick for confirmation. Derrick scrambled to keep the shock from his face. Being pregnant was something he should know… as her fiancé.

"Yes," he said. "She's pregnant."

"In that case, x-rays are out. How far along are you?"

"Umm, nearly 12 weeks," she replied.

The doctor wrote it down. "I think we better keep you in for observation overnight."

"Whatever you think necessary, doctor," Derrick answered.

10

Jacey half-listened as the nurse went through her prescriptions, as well as some instructions for her care. Derrick appeared to be hanging onto every word.

Everything leading up to her being in the hospital was still a bit of a blur. How had Derrick found her? Jacey looked around her. How had she ended up in a private room? She barely had enough money to cover the prescriptions, let alone the hospital bill.

"You need a lot of rest and care, Ms. Reynolds. The doctor is worried about how underweight you are, getting your body weight up is important. You need to discuss this with your own doctor and obstetrician."

"Don't worry, we will," Derrick said grimly.

Jacey turned to look at him. He hadn't said a word about her pregnancy. In fact, he hadn't said much at all. Derrick had insisted on staying with her the night, but Jacey had been so exhausted that she'd fallen asleep before she could question him.

This morning, the nurse had helped her get ready, while Derrick went to get some breakfast. What was he thinking? Why had he stayed with her? Why had he told them that he was her fiancé?

Derrick had taken care of everything, including filling out the paperwork. She wondered how he knew the last name she'd been using. Reynolds was her mother's maiden name. She hadn't told him that, had she? Then she remembered giving it to the policeman at the scene of Cece's accident. He must have overheard her. That was twice her name had appeared on paperwork. Not that Stephan would be looking for a Jacey Reynolds.

She hoped. Maybe it was time to move on. But she was so tired. She wanted to be safe. She had to be.

"All right, then. Get these prescriptions filled and I hope your pregnancy goes well. I'll get an orderly here to wheel you out."

Derrick took the paperwork, and Jacey smiled at the nurse as she bustled off.

"How are you doing, baby? Tired?"

"A bit," she replied. "Derrick, what are you doing here?"

He gazed at her for a long moment. "What do you mean?"

"Well." She glanced down at her hands, feeling embarrassed. "Why did you bring me to the hospital? Why did you stay the night? Why did you tell them I was your fiancée?"

He took her hand, running his thumb over her bare ring finger. "I told them that because I knew they wouldn't let me stay unless they thought I had a relationship with you."

"But we don't have a relationship. It was a one-night stand. I don't understand why you're here."

She coughed, and he reached for a glass of water, holding it up so she could take a few sips.

She leaned back against the raised bed, catching her breath. Derrick leaned forward, his gaze intently.

"Listen to me carefully, Jacey. You were not a one-night stand. I made a connection with you, and I know you felt the same. Even though you didn't answer my calls." His voice had a scolding note.

"My phone was stolen. I'm not good for you, Derrick."

"Stop that. You are perfect for me. I couldn't stop thinking about you while I was away, worrying about you. I only wish that I had asked you to stay at my place, maybe then you wouldn't have been wandering the streets, burning up with fever."

"I wasn't wandering the streets. I was searching for a job."

"I know, baby." He ran a cool hand over her forehead. "But you don't have to worry about that anymore. I'm here. I'm going to take care of you."

Although she should protest, right now it sounded like absolute bliss just to lie back and let someone else take all the worry and stress from her shoulders.

"All you need to do is concentrate on getting well and taking care of this baby."

He laid his hand on her stomach, his touch so gentle it brought tears to her eyes. What would it be like to have this man as the father of her baby? She knew that he would do anything to protect and take care of them.

"You haven't asked me who the father is," she said.

"Your ex?" he questioned.

"Yes."

"He's definitely out of your life?"

"I never want to see him again," she told him fervently.

Tension drifted from his shoulders. "Then it doesn't matter."

∼

JACEY STARED up at Derrick's house as he pulled the car up to the front door. She let out a small sigh as he jumped out of the car. Undoing her belt, she reached for her door handle. She'd tried to protest, but he'd brushed her arguments aside, telling her to sit back and rest.

To her chagrin, she'd done just that. It was just so easy to let Derrick take over. She knew it wasn't right. She had so many secrets, so many reasons why she couldn't get involved with him. But right now those reasons had flown out the window.

She just needed to catch her breath. She didn't want to take advantage of Derrick. As soon as she felt better, she'd leave.

Derrick opened her door and reaching in, scooped her up into his arms.

"Derrick! I can walk."

"Save your lungs, love. Besides, I like carrying you. You wouldn't deny me that pleasure, would you?"

Robert approached them as Derrick headed toward the front door. "Let me get the door for you."

"Thanks, Robert. Jacey, do you remember Robert?"

She nodded at the older man who smiled down at her.

"I'm going to take Jacey upstairs. She needs to rest. There are a few prescriptions sitting in the car, could you go get them filled for me? I'll be working from home for at least the rest of the week."

"Certainly. Hope you feel better soon, miss."

"Please, call me Jacey," she said with a smile.

Robert closed the door behind them, and Derrick carried her toward the stairs.

"Derrick, you don't have to rearrange your life for me," she said in protest. "I'll be perfectly fine here on my own."

"Baby, the best thing about being the boss is that I can do whatever suits me. And right now, what suits me best is to work from home so I can keep an eye on you."

He strode into his bedroom, and Jacey gave up arguing. Truth be told, she just didn't have the energy. Derrick sat her on the side of the bed, and Jacey looked around as he walked over to a chest of drawers.

"My backpack!" she said with relief. Derrick turned.

"Yes, you were wearing it when I found you. I brought it back here with me. I haven't opened it. I can unpack it if you like."

"No, that's okay," she told him, not wanting him to see that she carried her whole life in that bag.

She stood, swaying slightly as spots danced in front of her eyes. "Sit down before you fall down," he growled he placed a firm hand surrounded her nape as Derrick murmured to her soothingly.

"That's it, take another breath."

"I'm okay now," she said, coughing as he helped her sit up. Derrick reached over and poured a glass of water from the pitcher on the nightstand and held it up to her lips. Jacey sipped from it.

"You can unpack your backpack later after you've rested," he said.

What was it with her and take-charge men? Why couldn't she fall for an easy-going guy who would do what she said?

Because that wasn't what she wanted.

"Raise your arms."

"What?"

He held out some pajamas. They were silky and a deep crimson color. "I had Jenny, my housekeeper, do some shopping. Hold your arms up, and I'll help you get changed."

She blushed bright red. Seeing her naked during sex was one thing, but this was a whole different ball game. When had anyone taken care of her like this? Only her nanny when she was sick as a child. Her parents had never shown any interest and Stephan had always expected her to wait on him. Whether she was feeling up to it or not.

Derrick's behavior confused her.

"Jacey? What are you thinking?"

"Nothing," she replied automatically.

Derrick raised her face, his hand gentle but firm beneath her chin. "We're going to have to work on that, aren't we?"

"What?"

"On getting you to open up. When I ask a question, I don't want a brush off or to hear what you think I want to hear. I really want to know what you're thinking."

Jacey tried to move her head away, feeling uncomfortable. But Derrick tightened his hold. Not to the point of pain, but she knew he wasn't budging.

"I'm not used to doing that."

He chuckled. "I can tell. Would you like me to help you?"

She raised her gaze to his. Letting him into her head was dangerous, it opened the way for her secrets to spill out. But as she looked up into his gaze and saw the concern, she wanted to open up to him.

"Yes," she whispered. "But I'm not sure I should. I can't...there are things..." she trailed off, and he sat beside her, pulling her onto his lap.

"Let's just take this slow. At the moment you're not well, and my main goal is to get you feeling better. Let's concentrate on that for now, and we'll slowly work on getting you to open up and trust me."

She grabbed his hand. "I trust you more than anyone else I know."

He grinned, a smile that turned his face from handsome to breath-taking. Leaning in, he kissed her gently.

"Thank you, baby. Let's get you into bed, okay? You look knackered."

She smiled. Most of the time he sounded so American, then every so often his accent would become obvious, or he'd say a word like knackered, and his English heritage would slip through. It was sexy as hell.

Ignoring her protests that she could do it herself, he soon had her stripped and dressed in amazingly comfortable pajamas.

"You didn't have to buy me anything, Derrick."

"I wasn't sure what you had. There are more clothes in the dresser for when you're feeling better. Do you need to go to the bathroom?"

"Yes, but I can—Derrick!"

He swept her up, striding for the bathroom. Setting her down on her feet, he reached for her pajama bottoms. Jacey quickly slammed her hands down on his.

"Uh-uh, no way."

"Jacey—"

"No," she said firmly, before bending over as a cough wracked her body. Derrick held her close as she shook, running his hand up and down her back.

"Better?" he asked as she calmed.

She nodded her head, feeling exhausted. She leaned her head against his chest.

"I really need to go to the bathroom. Alone."

Derrick kissed her forehead. "Okay, I'll wait outside the door. Call me when you're finished, and I'll carry you back to bed."

Jacey used the toilet then washed her hands, glancing at herself in the mirror. She was pale, her cheeks overly pronounced with dark circles marring the skin beneath her eyes.

There was a knock on the door. "Jacey?"

"Ready," she called out.

Derrick opened the door, moving in to collect her up into his arms.

"You can't keep carrying me everywhere, Derrick," she told him, much as she enjoyed being in his arms.

He shrugged. "I can try."

The covers on the bed had been thrown back, and he tucked her in, pulling them back up and tucking them around her.

"And what about when I need to go to the bathroom while you're downstairs?"

He frowned, thinking. Then the lines on his face lightened, and he stood up, striding from the room.

What was he up to?

When he returned, he had something in his hands. Was that? No, it couldn't be.

"A baby monitor? Are you serious?" She gaped at him.

"I've been doing up a nursery for Holly's baby. Just got this the other day. I was thinking of how I could move my study up here, but that might disturb you. This is much better."

"Derrick! You are not using a baby monitor to keep an eye on me."

"Why not?"

He placed the monitor base on the nightstand and plugged it in. He held the receiver in his other hand.

"Ahh, maybe because I'm not a baby? What do you think I'm going to do? Cry when I want to go to the bathroom? Why don't you just put a diaper on me and stick me in a crib?"

"Not my kink, love."

She gaped at him, taking in his words.

"Just call out when you need something, and I'll help you downstairs." He held up the receiver.

"Do you seriously think I'm going to...wait, what do you mean, not your kink? Do you mean...?" Her face went bright red, and she felt suddenly very naïve as he winked at her.

"To each his own," he said. "And yes, I seriously expect you to call out if you need me. I don't want you going to the bathroom alone while you're still having dizzy spells."

She glared up at him, and he ran his finger over her cheek. "Disobey me on this and I will…" he trailed off.

"You'll what?" she asked, curious. Spank her? Tie her to the bed? Instead of scaring her as the thought should. Her pussy grew wet with excitement.

"I'll think of some punishment."

Leaning down, he kissed her on the forehead. When he stood up, Jacey felt a stab of disappointment. Her lips tingled, wanting his touch.

"Get some sleep, baby. I'll be back to check on you later. And call out for me if you need me." He gave her a stern look then left the room before she could reply. Jacey closed her eyes with a disgruntled sigh, wondering how she would ever sleep. In less than five minutes, she drifted off.

Derrick stood outside his bedroom, willing the erection pressing against his pants to die down. She was ill, for God's sake. He had no business fantasizing about tying her to his bed, her arms and legs spread wide while he feasted on her pussy.

He certainly had no business nearly threatening to spank her. Was he trying to terrify her? He knew she was scared to let him dominate her after what her ex had done.

He wanted to know more about her. Like what she was doing living on the streets? If her ex was the father of her baby, then she hadn't been separated from him as long as Derrick had thought.

She was ill, fragile and pregnant. She deserved his care and consideration, not an interrogation. He also needed to keep his hands to himself for a while, which was why he'd resisted taking her mouth in a deep, satisfying kiss.

Instead, he was slumped in the corridor, trying to cool his desire. He squeezed his cock through his pants. Christ, he was never going to get any work done this way. Moving to one of the guest bathrooms, he walked inside and turned on the water.

Stripping, he stepped inside, welcoming the chilly water against his overheated skin. He grabbed his erection in one hand, leaning the other hand against the side of the shower as he pumped his hand up and down his cock. Closing his eyes, he brought up the image of Jacey's naked body, her lips plump and swollen from his kisses, her pussy moist and waiting for his touch.

His balls tightened, a burning sizzled throughout his body, and he moved his hand faster, squeezing down on his dick as pleasure raced through him, blinding him with ecstasy. He opened his eyes as sperm shot out of his cock. Leaning heavily against his hand, he took in deep, cleansing breaths.

He was right to keep his hands off her, he was in control of his needs, not the other way around. Jacey needed care and attention at the moment. There was no way he intended to lose her.

No way would he make the same mistakes with her as he had with Cara.

11

"Does the name Jacey Reynolds mean anything to you?" Evan asked.

Stephan frowned for a minute, wondering if his brother had finally lost what was left of his twisted mind. "No, what possible interest could this woman be..." he quickly sat up, losing his irritation as his brain kicked into gear. He clenched the phone hard in his hand.

"Reynolds was Jacinta's mother's maiden name."

"And we have a winner." His brother let out a superior cackle, and Stephan took a deep breath to calm his temper, reminding himself that he needed his brother. "And Jacinta could easily be shortened to Jacey."

"So she's using this name."

"Looks that way. I did a bit of digging into who the man was in that photo with her."

Stephan's temper reared its head again at the memory of Jacey huddled against the other man. She was his, damn it. He forced his free hand to unclench as he took a deep breath.

"And? Who was he?"

"Derrick Ashdown. As in Ashdown resorts and hotels. Very rich."

Stephan blew out a breath. "What the hell is she doing with him? How did she meet him?"

"Looks like it might have been accidental. They both came across Cece's accident. But how they met is irrelevant. What is interesting is that he checked her into the hospital a few days ago."

"What? What's wrong with her?" Stephan didn't know how Evan got his information and frankly, he didn't want to know. If his brother ever got caught, he did not intend to go down with him. He needed to keep his reputation pristine if he was going to run for Governor.

"Looks like a case of bronchitis."

Stephan snorted. "Jacey never was strong."

"There's one more thing, something that could change everything. She's pregnant."

Stephan froze.

"How far along?"

"Twelve weeks."

Stephan dropped the phone.

∼

JACEY CLIMBED from the bed with a yawn. She stretched, feeling better than she had in a long time, even before contracting bronchitis. Amazing what sleeping in a comfortable bed and having plenty of food and very little stress could do for a woman.

While she was rubbing her eyes, she miscalculated as she walked around the edge of the bed and slammed her toes into the wooden bedpost leg of the bed.

"Aww, shoot. Oww, oww, oww." She hopped around on one foot, holding her throbbing toes with her hand. Tears welled in her eyes.

"What happened?"

She glanced up as Derrick rushed out of the master bathroom, a towel wrapped around his waist.

"What is it?" He rushed over and picked her up, sitting with her on his lap in the armchair.

"Nothing," she gritted out through clenched teeth. "Just stubbed my toes."

"Let me have a look." He didn't give her time to answer, just brushed away her hands to inspect her toes. "Can you wiggle them?"

"Yes, they're fine. I'm sorry for making such a fuss." She was embarrassed that she'd brought him running over some sore toes.

"Does this hurt?" He pressed down on each of her toes.

She hissed.

"Sorry, baby. We'd better take you in for an x-ray."

"What?" She gaped at him as he stood and carried her over to the bed, setting her down carefully.

"Just let me get dressed, and I'll run you into the emergency room." Derrick turned away.

Jacey shook her head. "Derrick, I stubbed my toes. They're fine. In five minutes I will have completely forgotten that I hurt them. I do not need an x-ray."

He turned to stare at her for a long moment. "Better to be safe than sorry."

"Derrick, no," she told him firmly. "No x-ray. I can't, remember." She placed her hand over her stomach. They rarely talked about the baby, and she couldn't help but wonder if he wanted to completely ignore the situation. He had no problem talking to her about any other aspect of her health, sometimes to an embarrassing degree.

He looked at her, his eyes filled with chagrin. "God, I forgot. Of course, you can't. But the doctor can look you over."

"Derrick, look, see they're fine." She wiggled her toes, doing her best to hide any pain. She had definitely whacked them hard. "No doctor, please."

"If they're still hurting later or show signs of swelling or bruising, I'm going to take you in to get them checked."

Jacey nodded. She knew the art of compromise.

Derrick's cell phone rang, and he picked it up, striding back into the bathroom. Jacey stood, walking over to the sofa by the fireplace. Derrick had even installed a television above the fireplace to keep her entertained. He'd even brought up a small refrigerator and had it stocked with drinks and snacks, so she didn't have to go up and down the stairs.

He'd thought of everything.

And yet... there was something missing. He no longer seemed to be attracted to her. She'd become a patient, a project for him and it seemed he'd stopped seeing her as a woman.

"I have to go into the office. There have been some problems with one of our projects, and I need to oversee some things personally."

"Sure, no problem," she said brightly, trying to ignore the fact that he never called her baby anymore.

"You going to watch a movie?"

"Maybe," she said with a smile.

"Well, don't walk around too much on those toes." He glanced over at the bed. "Maybe I should change the bed for something with soft edges."

"Don't you dare," she replied, looking at him in outrage. "I love that bed. I'm just clumsy, I'd probably smash my toes against an air mattress."

He smiled at her. "We'll see."

∼

JACEY STEPPED into the large living area of Derrick's house, glancing around in interest. She hadn't had a chance to do much exploring since she'd arrived eight days ago from the hospital.

With Derrick out of the house, she was taking the opportunity to stretch her legs. Plus, she was curious about Derrick's house. It wasn't snooping, she reassured herself. After all, she wasn't going to open up drawers or cupboards. She just wanted to get out of that bedroom for a while.

Derrick had done everything he could to make her feel at home. But she was feeling a lot better now, and she was starting to wonder if she was outstaying her welcome.

Derrick hadn't said anything, of course. But he hadn't touched her. Not sexually, anyway. And when he had, his touch had been fleeting and brief, almost as though he was afraid of catching something from her. It was a big difference from the man she'd spent the night with. Then he'd barely let her out of his arms.

He hadn't kissed her once. Not properly. He'd even taken to sleeping on the sofa. She should insist on moving into a spare bedroom. Although he'd remained conscientious about her health, he'd lost that stern edge to his voice. Surprisingly, she actually missed that side of him.

Had she done this with her inability to open up and trust? Maybe. Or maybe he just regretted bringing her home with him.

Stepping outside, she lay down on one of the poolside loungers, luxuriating in the feel of the sunshine on her skin.

Derrick didn't need her hanging around like a bad smell, keeping him from his work and probably from socializing as well. A stab of jealousy hit her at the thought of him with other women, but she had no right to feel that way. He wasn't hers. If she stayed too much longer, she'd never be able to leave. Yes, leaving was best. For both of them.

∽

"Jacey?" Derrick called out, thinking she must be in the bathroom when he didn't find her curled up on the sofa or in bed.

"Jacey?" He knocked on the bathroom door. When there was no reply, he opened the door. Empty. Panic unfurled, and he pushed it down. He'd only been gone four hours. She must be in another part of the house. He shook his head.

She knew he didn't want her wandering up and down the stairs by herself. Although she was a lot better, there was still a slight wheeze to her breathing, and he didn't want her testing her lungs. If she had a coughing fit halfway down the stairs or felt dizzy, she could fall and be seriously hurt.

"Jacey, where are you? Answer me now." He grew increasingly concerned as he wandered through the house. Then he saw that one of the French doors in the living room was open. Stepping outside, he spotted her on one of the sun loungers.

"What are you doing out here?"

"What? Huh?" She sat up, looking confused. "Derrick? You're back quick. Did you forget something?"

"I've been gone four hours," he said, unable to tone down the sternness in his voice. "What were you doing sleeping out here? You could have gotten burned."

"My skin doesn't really burn." She stood, swaying slightly.

Derrick immediately scooped her up in his arms. "You're dizzy. Bloody hell, do you know what could have happened if you'd had a dizzy spell on the stairs? You could have broken your neck!"

"Derrick," she said softly, placing her hand on his cheek. "I'm fine. I just stood up too quickly."

"You know I don't want you wandering around the house alone." He carried her through the living room and set her on the sofa. Sitting on the coffee table across from her, he picked up her foot, testing the toes she'd stubbed earlier.

"I wasn't snooping," she said sharply.

He glanced up at her, his gaze narrowing. "I don't recall saying that. I'm worried about you hurting yourself while you're alone in the house. How are your toes?"

"They're fine." She slipped her toes from his grasp. "Derrick, I need to talk to you."

"Yes?" he said, not liking the serious tone to her voice.

"I think it's time I left."

"What?"

"I can't stay here forever. I'm feeling a lot better, and I can't thank you enough for everything you've done, but I can't help but feel that it's time to move on."

"Why?"

She looked at him in confusion. "You knew I'd have to leave sometime."

"And where exactly are you going to go, Jacey?" he said in a cold voice. "Should I just let you pack your bag and drop you off at the closest shelter?"

Jacey looked at Derrick in shock. He knew? How the hell did he know?

"How long have you known?"

"Since the day I returned from my trip and found out you'd been fired from the diner. I can't believe you wouldn't tell me."

He ran his hand through his hair, sending strands off at crazy angles.

"Oh, and what did you expect me to say? Thanks for the sex, Derrick. By the way, I'm homeless."

"You should have told me." His eyes looked haunted as he stared at her. "Do you think I would have just dropped you off the next morning if I'd known? You think I wouldn't have done everything I could to help you?"

"You're a good guy, Derrick. Probably the best guy I've ever met. But you can't solve everyone's problems."

"I don't want to solve everyone's problems. I'm not the good guy you think I am, Jacey. I can be ruthless when I need to be. I don't take in strays. I don't invite just anyone to live under my roof. I told you this before, but it obviously didn't get through to you. I care about you, Jacey. When I'm not with you, I can't stop thinking about you. Those days when I couldn't find you were some of the worst in my life. I imagined all sorts of horrible things, like you lying in a pool of blood in a dark alley with your throat slit."

He stared at her, his eyes haunted, his face pale. She felt a stab of guilt, which was crazy. She hadn't lied. And yet, she could see the torture he'd been through. How would she have felt if the tables were reversed?

"I need to keep you safe and healthy. And that most definitely means that you are not going out to live on the streets again."

"Derrick, listen to me. You can't just keep me, like a pet. I'm a grown woman with my own mind. I can make my own decisions."

"And you think going back to the way your life was before is a good decision? Particularly when you've barely recovered from bronchitis and pregnant? Just where are you planning on having this baby, Jacey? In an alley between two dumpsters?"

Jacey gasped, standing to glare down at him. "How dare you! Don't you think I've been saving every possible penny I can for this baby? I just need to find another job, start saving again and by the time the baby comes, I'll be set to pay for the hospital bill and rent us a small place for a while." *Maybe.* Sometimes the stress of worrying about her future became too much. If she thought about it all the time, she'd go mad. She just had to keep putting one foot in front of the other.

"You were seriously saving money on the peanuts you got paid at the diner?" he asked incredulously. "What were you doing working there anyway? You're obviously smart and educated, why weren't you working somewhere where you could make more money, maybe even get some health insurance?"

"None of your business. This child isn't yours, Derrick and neither am I. I'm grateful for everything you've done for us, but it's time I left now."

Ignoring her guilt at the flash of hurt in his eyes, Jacey turned away to walk from the room.

"Stop, Jacey," his deep voice commanded.

She paused, cursing herself for her instinctive reaction. Turning, she glared at him.

"Come here."

"Screw you!" Well, that was pathetic.

He walked toward her, like a predator cornering his prey. Jacey bit her lip as he stepped behind up her, unable to stop the surge of excitement. There was something so tantalizing about him. Irresistible.

His scent surrounded her as he gathered her hair up in one hand. He tugged her hair, making her gasp at the sting of pain which quickly morphed into a deep pleasure.

Derrick pulled her head over to one side, exposing her neck. Jacey closed her eyes as he laid soft kisses down her neck and over the exposed skin of her shoulder.

How did he do this to her? A few touches and she melted in his hands.

"Open your eyes," he demanded as he let go of her hair and moved around to face her. "Look at me."

Jacey gazed up into his face.

Cupping her cheeks, he tilted her head back and took her mouth in a deep kiss that soon had her knees weakening. She swayed when he drew back.

"I want you to watch me, to know who is touching you."

"Derrick—"

"No." He placed a finger over her mouth. "No talking unless I ask you a direct question. Do you believe I would hurt you?"

Swallowing heavily, she shook her head. "Not intentionally."

His gaze narrowed. "But you do think I'll hurt you?"

She glanced away. "I can't do this, Derrick. I can't give you what you want and lose who I am in the process. I won't be a mindless slave, catering to your every whim."

"What makes you think that I want that?" he asked.

"You like to be in control."

"In the bedroom, yes. But you want that too. I can see it in your face, the way you react to my commands. But I don't want a mindless slave. I love your feisty side. There will be times I push you outside the bedroom. There will be times when I will win. But I know you have your own mind. I respect you. Never think that I don't."

He ran his hands over her shoulders, cupping her breasts. "I'm more trouble than I'm worth," she whispered.

"That's for me to decide, don't you think?"

"You don't know everything."

"But you're going to tell me."

"Do you really think you can keep from bossing me around outside the bedroom?" she asked dryly.

He grinned wickedly. "I don't believe I ever promised that. Just that I didn't expect you to blindly do as you're told. Although that would have its advantages."

She snorted.

Derrick cupped her cheek, running his thumb over her lips. "I want you here, Jacey. Whatever you tell me won't change that. I want to help you, to take care of you, and yeah, to dominate you."

Grabbing hold of her hand, he drew her over to the sofa, drawing her onto his lap.

"Talk to me, Jacey. Tell me what's going on with you."

She remained silent, not knowing where to even begin.

"You know, I haven't felt this way toward a woman since my wife died," Derrick told her.

"Your wife?" Her eyes widened. He'd never mentioned a wife before.

Derrick nodded, gazing out the window. "It's been nearly twenty years now since she died. Cara was so young. Naïve and vulnerable. I didn't take care of her as I should have and she died because of my carelessness. I couldn't stand if something like that happened to you, Jacey."

Well, that explained his overprotectiveness. He obviously still carried the guilt of his wife's death.

"I don't expect anything from you, Jacey. I don't want you to feel indebted to me, or like you owe me. The last thing I want is to have you fear me. I just have this need to take care of you. Can you let me do that?"

"So you're trying to appease your guilt over what happened to her by helping me?" she asked, trying to understand. Her head was starting to ache from it all.

"No...well, partly. I loved Cara, and I failed her. I won't fail you."

"But you don't love me."

He gazed down at her. "Maybe not yet. But I care about you in a way I have for no one else since Cara."

"But you haven't touched me since I arrived!" she protested. "You haven't kissed me or held me."

He looked at her incredulously. "Because you've been ill. Plus, I wanted to build up your trust in me."

"So you're still attracted to me?"

"I've had more cold showers in the last week than in my entire life! Of course, I'm still attracted to you, do you think that just disappears?"

She dropped her gaze. "I thought maybe the pregnancy had turned you off. Not every man would be attracted to a woman carrying another man's child."

"Look at me."

He waited until she raised her gaze to his. "This baby isn't just a part of him. It's a part of you, too. How could anything that is a part of you turn me off?"

Wow, he always knew just what to say.

"Jacey, tell me why you were living on the streets. Tell me what happened with your husband."

Part of her wanted to hold back to protect herself, the other part wanted to share her burden.

"I was an idiot. That's what happened."

"Jacey," he said in a low voice.

She sighed. "All right, I'll tell you. It's just where do I start?"

"Try the beginning."

"Well, in the beginning, everything was so good. I thought that he was perfect for me. The fact that he was into BDSM was both scary and exciting. We'd had this whirlwind relationship. Some of my friends warned me that it was too quick. That I should slow down, but I didn't listen to them. I loved him. Or I figured I did."

"What did he do to you?" Derrick asked in a tight voice.

Jacey lifted her head from his chest. "Are you sure you want to know?"

Derrick tilted her head up, staring down at her. "Tell me. I have to know."

"He started to change. It was little things at first. He got mad because I was late home or didn't tell him where I was going. He became more demanding. Little things would set him off. I told myself it was stress. I made excuses.

"Then one night I was at one of his work functions, chatting to a younger business associate. Stephan was all smiles and charm until we got home. He slapped me so hard that I feel backward and hit my head. I woke up cold, dazed and unsure where I was. I couldn't move. I was tied face down on the bed. He had my arms tied above my head, my legs spread-eagled and tied to the bed. Stephan appeared just as I was about to scream, he yanked my jaw open and stuffed a ball gag into my mouth. I hated being gagged. Of course, he did a lot of things I hated that night."

"Like what?"

"There was the flogger, which I'd always enjoyed, but this one was much rougher, coarser, then he moved on to a paddle then the whip," she shuddered. She hated that whip. "I wasn't into pain. I finally reached a place where the pain didn't even seem to reach me anymore like my body had gone into overload."

She swallowed hard.

"Oh, baby."

She felt Derrick tremble. Was he disgusted? Did he want her to stop?

"Did he rape you?"

She shook her head. "No, he, ahh, ejaculated over me." But there had been other times. Times when he'd taken her when she didn't want him. Not that she'd tried to stop him. She'd been too scared.

"He told me I was his. That I wasn't allowed to flirt with other guys, touch them, and that I was his only to do with what he liked. He untied me after that, told me to go wash up and get into bed. Do you know what? I did just that. I was so numb, in so much pain, I just washed up and curled up in bed."

"Oh, Jacey, you can't blame yourself for that." He hugged her tight. "Christ, I'm just so glad you left him after that. I hope you pressed charges."

She shook her head. She couldn't tell him the truth. That she'd been too scared to leave him, frightened because she had nowhere to go. She'd known her parents wouldn't help her and she had no real friends. So she'd stayed, until the day she'd discovered just how much of a monster he was.

"Stephan has friends in high places. The charges wouldn't stick."

"So he's out there? Free? What's his last name?"

"Whoa." She sat up and stared down at him. "No way."

"No way, what?"

"No way am I telling you his last name. You are not going after him."

He raised an eyebrow. "I assure you, I can take care of him. Quickly and quietly."

Jacey frantically shook her head. "You don't understand, Stephan is powerful, he could ruin you. No, I'm not telling you anything more. Besides, you said it didn't matter, remember?"

Derrick smiled. "That was before you told me all of this. Are you trying to protect me, love? There's really no need. I promise that I can look after myself."

Jacey crossed her arms over her naked chest. "Uh-uh, no way am I telling you."

He stared at her for a long moment but didn't push her. "Does he know about the baby?"

Jacey bit her lip. How much should she tell him?

"Jacey, does the father know?"

"No," she whispered. "And he can't know. He can't ever find us."

"You're hiding from him. That's why you worked at the diner because they paid in cash."

"Yes."

"Is Jacey Reynolds your real name?"

"No. Jacey is a name one of my nanny's used to call me. I always liked it. Reynolds is my mother's maiden name."

"Are you scared that if he finds you, he'll try to take the baby?" Derrick asked seriously.

"He cannot find out about the baby. I know he's looking for me. He won't let me go." She shook uncontrollably.

"Shh," he told her, running his hand through her hair. "You have me to protect you now. No way am I going to let him near you."

"He's very powerful, Derrick."

"Who is he?"

"Please don't ask me that. I can't tell you. It's too dangerous. For both of us."

She would never forgive herself if something happened to Derrick because of her. If Stephan found out where she was, he wouldn't hesitate to kill Derrick.

What had she been thinking, agreeing to stay here?

"Derrick," she began, looking up at him urgently. "I think I should lea–"

He placed a finger against her mouth. "Don't even think about it. I'm willing to let you keep his name a secret. For the moment. But only because you've had enough upsets lately. However, you will not try and protect me by leaving. That is unacceptable. I'm not without my own power and resources."

"You can't take the risk," she told him.

He stared down at her arrogantly. "That's my decision to make, not yours."

"Derrick, I don't know if I could ever if I could ever be with..."

"If you could ever submit? Ever fully trust again?"

She nodded.

"Honey, I would never do anything to scare you. Ever."

She could never ask him to sacrifice such a large part of his life for her, though.

"But don't let what he did ruin something you wanted, that you dreamed about. You're safe here. Tell me what you've dreamed about. Tell me what you desire. Before he showed his true colors was there anything you liked?"

Jacey took a deep breath and thought back to before Stephan became abusive. She shifted on Derrick's lap, tapping her fingers against her thigh. Derrick covered her hand with one of his.

"Well?"

"I guess, umm, do we really have to talk about this? I mean, I feel like I'm laying myself bare here."

He was silent for a long moment. "Fair enough. You tell me this, and then I'll tell you something about myself."

Curiosity filled her.

"Being tied up. I had liked it before Stephan showed his true side. Tied up and blindfolded." She blushed as she spoke.

"Very good, and what else?"

She cleared her throat. "I guess I was attracted to how Stephan took charge. In the beginning, you know, before he became violent and demanding."

He nodded.

"What else have you dreamed about? What toys turn you on?"

"Derrick," she protested.

"Vibrators?"

She nodded.

"Nipple clamps? Anal plugs."

She groaned but nodded again. Oh Lord, her cheeks were burning.

"Anything else, baby?"

"Umm, well I thought I liked the flogger. Stephan changed that." She shuddered at the memory.

He ran his hand up and down her back. "What about spankings? Did you ever enjoy those?"

She shook her head, burying her face against his chest.

"Oh no?"

"No," she replied firmly.

"You wouldn't be lying to me, would you, Jacey? Because I can check."

"Spankings hurt, they're not fun at all."

"Have you never dreamed of getting an erotic spanking, Jacey? Or about being turned over a knee and having your butt paddled as punishment for being a naughty sub? Hmm?"

"No!"

"Shall we test that? Spread your legs."

"Derrick," she moaned.

"Jacey," he said more firmly. "Spread your legs now."

She was wearing one of the long, flowing skirts he'd bought her and he easily pushed the material up to her waist to reveal her soaked panties.

"Pink panties, very pretty." He cupped her mound. Jacey was grateful that she'd shaved in the shower this morning as he pulled her panties to the side and dipped a finger into her soaking wet pussy.

"Hmm, very wet."

Embarrassed, she attempted to close her legs.

Derrick kept his hand where it was, turning his face to look at her sternly.

"Jacey. Part your legs."

Oh God, that voice. The command had her slowly opening her thighs.

"Good girl."

Her heart lightened, and she relaxed slightly. He ran his finger up her slit, tapping it against her swollen clit, circling it, tapping it, circling it again.

Jacey leaned her head against his shoulder, her breath coming faster as she moaned softly.

"Wait until you have permission, Jacey," he told her.

A low whimper escaped as she tried to gain some control over herself. Then he thrust a thick finger inside her, and she clenched around him as he used his thumb to manipulate her clit.

"Derrick, please," she cried.

"Tell me how that feels," he demanded.

"Good."

He chuckled. "You'll have to do better than that if you want to come."

She groaned in protest. "I can't."

"Yes, you can. Open up to me, Jacey. How do you feel? What do you like? Do you like having my finger inside you?"

"Yes," she cried. "But I want more."

"More? Two fingers?" He pushed another finger inside, and she thrust her hips up.

"Yes, please. Move them."

"Like this?" He drove them in and out of her passage. "Or like this?" Curling his fingers, he brushed them against a sensitive spot inside her that almost had her coming instantly.

He laughed again, and the sound of his happiness had her opening her eyes to stare up at him. She grinned.

"Both," she told him. "I like both. A lot. But I prefer having you inside me."

He shook his head. "Not this time. This time is all for you. Are you feeling hot?"

She nodded her head. "I'm on fire. I want more. I want to come. Please make me come." This wasn't her. This wasn't the demure woman her mother had raised. But Jacey didn't want to be that girl anymore.

The new Jacey was bold, daring.

"I need to come, Derrick. Don't make me wait."

"Then come."

Leaning in, he took her mouth in a deep kiss as his thumb flicked her clit furiously. The tips of his fingers brushed against her insides, making her shake. His tongue continued to play with hers, his mouth capturing her cry of rapture as she came.

He pressed down firmly on her clit, prolonging her orgasm as her passage continued to pulsate around him.

Finally, she collapsed against him, completely sated.

Derrick licked her essence from his fingertips and her clit throbbed at the erotic sight.

Once she'd regained her breath, she snuggled in against him, running her finger over his chest. "Tell me something about you."

"What would you like to know?" he asked.

"Tell me about your family. Do you have any siblings? Parents?"

"Both of my parents are dead. I barely remember my father and my mother died when I was eighteen. I have a younger brother, Matt. He's an asshole. The only good thing he ever did was marry Holly. He treated her abominably."

Jacey knew how close he and Holly were.

"You don't have anything to do with him?"

"No. Holly was in a bad accident a few years ago and hurt her leg badly. She was facing a long road of therapy and recovery. My asshole brother visited her in the hospital to tell her he wanted a divorce."

"That's terrible."

"Probably the best thing that could have happened. I moved her in with me, arranged for all her therapy. While she was recovering, she started working for me as my personal assistant. She still does."

"She lives in Austin?"

"No, she and Brax live near Waco. She works from home a lot."

"You must miss her."

"We talk most days. She's very important to me. Closer to me than my brother ever was."

Jacey wondered what Holly would think of her.

"She'll like you," Derrick said as if sensing her worry.

"She might think I'm using you."

"Nobody who meets you could think that," he told her. "Holly's a great person. Trust me. You two will get on great."

12

Jacey woke from her nap with a yawn. These days it felt like all she did was sleep and eat. Derrick had encouraged that throughout the two weeks she'd now been living here. Sitting, she rose from the bed slowly, knowing from experience that getting up too quickly would often result in a head rush.

Entering the bathroom, she used the facilities before washing her face to freshen up. Heading back into the bedroom, she got dressed. Just as she was moving toward the door, it opened, and Derrick walked in.

"Ahh, thought you might be up," he said.

Jacey placed her hands on her hips. "All right, where is it?"

"Where is what?" he asked, his eyes wide with innocence.

"The baby monitor," she said, walking around the room to look for it. Where had he hidden it? She'd made him remove the one he'd tried to install earlier. But there had been too many coincidences where he would turn up just as she started moving around. There had to be another monitor.

Hell, he probably had a half dozen of them. The nursery he'd set up for Holly's baby was overflowing with stuff he'd bought. He truly adored his sister-in-law, and Jacey got the feeling that Holly's baby would be spoiled rotten.

Jacey placed her hand over her stomach, thinking about everything she couldn't afford to buy her own baby. But it would be loved and protected. She would do everything she could to ensure that.

"What's wrong?" Derrick asked, placing his hand over hers. "Is it the baby? Are you in pain?"

"What? Oh no, I'm fine. Just thinking."

"About what?" he asked.

"Nothing."

Derrick turned her toward him. He drew her closer, kissing her softly.

"Want to rethink that answer, sweetheart? We don't have a lot of time before your doctor's appointment, but I think I can squeeze in enough time to get you nicely hot and bothered before we get there. Could make the car ride over very interesting."

She blushed. "You wouldn't!"

He stared at her calmly. Oh God, he would. There had been a few times in the past week where she'd brushed off his questions with vague answers. She'd soon learned how serious he was about her talking to him.

He was so devious. Each time she'd brushed him off, he would take her to the point of completion then refuse to allow her orgasm. The one time she'd tried to take matters into her own hands, he'd tied her hands with silken ropes behind her back then started all over again.

She'd soon got the message.

"No, don't," she cried as he raised her t-shirt. "I'll talk! I'll talk! You should have been an interrogator."

He chuckled but kept his hands cupped over her breasts. "I don't think the Geneva Convention would approve of my techniques."

"No, it goes above and beyond. I think a spanking would be less torturous."

"Just say the word, beautiful," he told her, his voice growing thick with desire. She glanced down at his pants where his erection pressed against them firmly.

She licked her lips.

He'd promised not to spank her until she was ready. Only the more he mentioned it, the hotter she grew.

"Damn it, Jacey. Don't look at me like that. We don't have time for a spanking or play. I don't think you want to go the doctor with a red ass. Tell me."

Jacey drew in a deep breath. "I was just thinking about everything I can't give this baby."

His gaze narrowed and she carried on quickly before he thought she was greedy.

"But I can give him or her a lot of love. And protection. I know that it's just..." she trailed off.

"I don't want you worrying about what you can and can't buy for this baby. You know this baby won't want for anything, don't you?"

"Derrick, you can't just buy us whatever we need."

"Why not?" He looked confused.

"Because...because I feel like I'm using you. You won't even let me repay you by doing anything around here."

"I pay people to do that," he said arrogantly. "Would you do them out of a job?"

"Of course not!" she replied indignantly. "I just wish I felt like I was contributing."

He watched her for a moment. "Did you know that I grew up poor?"

"What? No." He'd shared very little of himself with her. Not that she could complain, there were still some things she'd kept from him. For his own good, she justified, although she felt guiltier by the day for holding back.

He nodded. "Some days we barely had food on the table. My mother worked two jobs just to keep a roof over our heads. She worked herself into an early grave. I always vowed that my children wouldn't grow up in poverty, that my wife wouldn't work herself half to death." There was sorrow in his eyes.

Her breath caught. "Derrick–"

"Then I let my wife do just that. Cara was so tired from working hard all day that she fell asleep on the bus and missed our stop. She didn't want to pay for another ride, so she walked back from the stop she'd got off at. Three men jumped her, pulled her into an alley. They raped and killed her."

Jacey was speechless.

"I should have been there to meet her at the bus stop each night. I should have demanded that she not work so hard. But we had very little money, and she insisted. Cara died because I couldn't take care of her."

"No, Derrick, that's not true."

He watched her with hard eyes. "But I can take care of you and this baby. If you'll let me."

"Oh, Derrick, you already take good care of us. We don't need your money as well."

"What good is my money, if it doesn't protect and care for the people I love?"

"Y-you love me?"

Ignoring her question, he glanced at his watch. "We'd better go. We'll be late."

∼

JACEY GLANCED over at Derrick as she sat on the examination table. He sat in a chair across the room, the look on his face pensive. The car ride over had been silent.

He loved her? Did he mean it? Was he regretting saying it and that's why he'd gone silent? Maybe he'd been remembering how much he loved Cara and his feelings had spilled over onto her. No, that was ridiculous. Wasn't it?

"Hello." The doctor walked in, a friendly, older man. Derrick had arranged the appointment, so she knew he must be very good.

"You must be Jacey." He walked over and shook her hand. "And Derrick." He moved to Derrick who stood and shook his hand.

"Thanks for fitting us in, doctor," Jacey said. Derrick hadn't been happy that they'd had to wait until now to see him. He must have pulled a few strings just to get her in.

"Not a problem. I'm only sorry I couldn't fit you in earlier. After everything your fiancé has done for this hospital, it was the least we could do." He flipped open her file.

"I have your records from the hospital. How are you feeling after having bronchitis? Still coughing?"

She shook her head. "No, I feel fine."

He asked a whole range of questions. His nurse had already taken her vitals, and he discussed the need to raise her body weight. Derrick remained silent, but she knew he was taking in each word.

"Well, how about we do an ultrasound?"

Jacey nodded.

"Lie back." He squirted some gel on her tummy after lowering her jeans.

Derrick came over to her side, and Jacey held out her hand, grateful when he took it. She couldn't help but feel nervous, worried they might find something wrong with the baby.

"And there is your baby."

Jacey let out a soft gasp. In grainy black and white, there was her baby. The doctor took some measurements while Jacey just stared at the baby growing inside her.

"There we go, two arms, two legs, and everything looks fine. We'll do some blood tests too and get you back here in a few weeks. But at the moment, other than making sure you get plenty of good food and rest I don't anticipate any issues."

He wiped the gel off her stomach.

"Thank you," Jacey said as the printer spat out two images of her baby.

"You're welcome." The doctor smiled as Derrick helped her up, and guided her to the door. "Speak to reception on the way out."

Before they left, they made another appointment. As they walked to the car, Jacey bit her lip.

Derrick helped her into the car, before moving around to his own seat.

"What is it?" he asked.

"Hmm?"

"You're worrying about something. You've gone very quiet."

"So have you," she accused. "Are you angry with me?"

Shocked, he stared at her. "Angry? No, why?"

"You seem angry. I know you didn't mean it when you said you loved me, you were just thinking about Cara-"

He clasped her cheeks between his hands, and she grew quiet. "You listen to me. I was not thinking of Cara. I mean, I was, but not when I told you I love you. I love you, Jacey."

"Really?" she whispered.

"Really."

"I love you, too."

"Then you'll let me look after you and the baby," he said with firmly. "If you're mine, this baby is mine. I will claim it as mine. Unless you don't want that."

She took a deep breath. "Are you sure?"

"Oh yes."

She leaned over, throwing her arms around him. He kissed her. "You're going to make a great daddy."

He grinned. "I like the sound of that."

"It's costing you a lot of money, though, me not having health insurance and everything."

"Like I said before, my money means nothing if I can't use it to look after you. Besides, once we're married you'll have all the health care and insurance you could ever need."

"You want to marry me?" Things were moving rather fast.

"Well, this isn't exactly how I thought to propose. But yes, I want you and this baby to have my name."

"We can't get married, though, because if I file for a divorce, then he'll know where I am."

"I want to marry you. I want you and this baby to carry my name.

I know you must be worried he'll file for custody but I won't allow that. I will find everything I need to protect you and this baby."

"You just don't understand, Derrick. You don't know what he's like. The lengths he's capable of going to."

"Because you won't talk to me. Tell me. I won't allow him near you. Look, Jacey, I know you're terrified, but you can't live like this forever. You have to trust that I will take care of you and the baby."

"I know you think I'm overreacting, that I'm being silly–"

"He terrorized you, abused you, it's okay to be afraid, Jacey. But the sooner we do this, the sooner you can see that he can't hurt you anymore."

"Damn it, Derrick, will you just listen to me!"

Derrick stared at her in shock, and she was a bit surprised by the anger in her voice.

"I am not being over-dramatic. I am not making him out to be worse than he is. While I remain hidden, we're safe, you, me and the baby. If he finds out where I am, he won't hesitate to kill us."

13

"So do you have a plan?" Stephan asked his brother impatiently, clenching his hand around his phone.

"We're watching Ashdown's house around the clock. We'll get her eventually."

"Eventually isn't good enough," Stephan said angrily. "Just go in there and grab her."

"He's got a shitload of security. I'm sure we can get around it, but we go in without a plan, and we're done for. If you don't think I'm doing a good job, you could come here and grab her yourself, brother," Evan said silkily, and Stephan knew he'd crossed a line with his stepbrother.

"Evan, I'm sorry," Stephan said, injecting his voice with just the right amount of apology. "Of course you know your job, I'm just impatient to get my hands on her."

"You're not the only one in deep shit if she speaks, Stephan," Evan said.

"You're right." Only Evan didn't stand to lose nearly as much as Stephan did. He was a nobody. Oh, there would be some backlash on Stephan, but he could spin it into his favor. Stephan had witnesses lined up, prepared to swear that Evan's issues stemmed from abuse suffered prior to his moving in with Stephan's father. No way was Stephan going down for his assistant's death. No way in hell.

He was willing to get rid of anybody who stood in his way, including his wife. So far, he'd managed to hide her absence by telling everyone she'd gone to Europe on vacation. But that excuse wouldn't last forever.

"You realize taking Ashdown out isn't going to be that easy," Evan said. "I've been looking into him, he's got a lot of powerful connections. If Jacinta tells him the truth, he could ruin you."

"She won't tell him. She knows he's a dead man if she does."

Evan chuckled. "Too bad she doesn't know he's a dead man either way."

∼

"Derrick, that nursery puts ours to shame."

Jacey raised her head as Derrick's handsome brother-in-law stepped into the living room, his arm around his pretty wife, Holly.

Somehow, they weren't quite what she'd expected. She'd had a picture in her mind of Holly being tall, slim and dressed in designer clothes with perfect make-up and hair.

Instead, she was quite normal looking. Her long, dark hair was tied back in a loose ponytail. She wore casual black pants and a pink shirt. Jacey knew Holly had injured her leg in a car accident, but she couldn't detect a limp.

Her husband, Brax, was gorgeous. He had that whole cowboy thing going on, even though Derrick said he was in construction. His gray gaze didn't miss much, but his eyes warned when he looked at his wife.

Derrick walked into the room behind them. Brax led Holly over to the sofa opposite the one Jacey sat on.

"I asked the lady in the store to give me the best of everything that I needed," Derrick said as he poured sparkling water into wine glasses and handed one first to Holly then to Jacey. As her fingers brushed his, she shivered.

Things had been strained between them since her refusal to tell him who Stephan was.

Telling him would only place him in danger. He would insist on fixing it, and that would bring him into Stephan's radar.

What if Stephan does find me, what then?

She pushed away the disturbing thought, tuning in to the conversation as Holly told Derrick off for buying all that nursery gear. Brax watched on with amusement, taking the beer Derrick offered him.

Derrick then sat next to her on the sofa. She smiled over at him.

"So how did the two of you meet?" Holly asked in a friendly voice.

"Oh, well, we actually met when Cece had crashed her car a few weeks ago," Jacey replied.

"Oh." Holly's eyes widened as she stared over at Derrick and Jacey frowned slightly in puzzlement at her reaction. Was there something significant about Cece's accident?

Derrick reached over and grabbed her free hand, giving it a squeeze. "I told Holly about meeting this amazing woman at Cece's accident and how I couldn't get her out of my head."

"Oh." Jacey blushed at the idea that he'd wanted her even then.

"I advised him to try and find you. I've never seen Derrick so taken with anyone," Holly told her. "I'm glad he found you."

"Thanks."

Jacey started to relax. She'd been nervous about meeting Holly and Brax, scared about what they might think about her, but so far things were going pretty smoothly.

"So, Jacey, where do you work?"

"Umm, well, I just got laid off, unfortunately."

"Oh no, that's terrible," Holly said. "The economy is terrible at the moment. I can't imagine how hard it must be searching for a new job."

"Jacey's not worrying about that at the moment," Derrick interjected with a firm look at her. "She's been ill. So she's taking it easy and concentrating on looking after herself and her baby."

"Oh, you have a child?"

"No, umm, I'm pregnant." She could kick Derrick. She shot him a look out of the corner of her eye. What would they think of her now?

"How far along are you? Is it yours?" Holly directed the last question to Derrick.

Derrick let out a snort of laughter. "I'd have to be a pretty fast worker. Jacey is about fourteen weeks along, and her ex is the biological father."

"Wow, seriously. I'm in shock," Holly said. "This seemed to happen very quickly. And you don't even look like you're showing; while here I am at eleven weeks, already bulging out of my clothes like a fat piggy."

"Holly," Brax reprimanded sharply, while Derrick frowned at his sister-in-law.

Brax gently grabbed his wife chin, turning her face towards his. "We've talked about you putting yourself down," he said in a soft voice that was nevertheless filled with command.

"Sorry, Sir," she whispered. Jacey sucked in a deep breath. Brax was a Dom, she was sure of it. She stared at Holly, the other woman certainly seemed happy enough. Even now, with all of Brax's focus on her as he reprimanded her, she looked back at him with love.

"Good girl." He kissed her cheek.

"I actually wish I was showing a bit more," Jacey told Holly.

"Guess we always want what we don't have, huh?" Holly leaned against Brax.

"So you see, you don't need to scold me for buying so much stuff," Derrick said. "There will be two babies to use it all." He placed a hand over Jacey's stomach, and she stiffened in surprise at his touch.

"I'm not sure whether just replicating the nursery in another room wouldn't be better, though, because we'll probably want this baby's nursery a bit closer to our room, won't we?" he asked Jacey.

She opened and closed her mouth. "Umm."

"Wait, our room? You mean, Jacey lives here? With you?" Holly looked at them in shock.

"Yes, that's right."

"But you two barely know each other."

"Holly," Brax said in a low, warning voice.

"Wait, so she doesn't have a job, she's pregnant with someone else's child, and she's living with you? Derrick, do you know what you're doing? Have you made her sign an agreement?"

"Holly!" Brax warned in a sharper tone. "That's enough. This is Derrick's life, it's up to him how he wants to live it."

"But–"

"But nothing. I think you owe Derrick and Jacey an apology, don't you?"

Holly just glared at him.

"No, she doesn't. At least, not to me." Jacey sat forward. "Holly, maybe you and I could talk in private for a moment?"

Jacey hated confrontation, she'd normally run in the other direction, happy to let someone else deal with the issue. But Holly was important to Derrick, and she wanted to get along with the other woman. So she needed to convince Holly that she had Derrick's best interests in mind.

"Fine."

Holly stood then followed Jacey out of the room.

Jacey led them out onto the deck. "Look, Holly, I know what you must be thinking. I'd be thinking the exact same thing if I were in your shoes. You love Derrick, and you want to protect him. Well, so do I."

She took a deep breath and looked out over the beautiful grounds. "Believe it or not I've tried to leave. I told Derrick that I didn't want to take advantage of him. Derrick wouldn't even consider it. I had my mind made up, and in the space of ten minutes, he had me promising to stay here and let him look after me."

Holly snorted. Jacey turned to look at her, thinking the other woman thought she was lying. "I really did."

"Oh, you probably did. I know what Derrick's like. He's nearly as bad as Brax in the bossy male department."

Actually, Jacey thought Derrick probably had Brax beat in that department. But she didn't want to argue with Holly.

"I would sign whatever Derrick wanted me to, Holly. I know you don't know me, but the very last thing I want is to take advantage of Derrick. He's, well, he's very important to me."

"I love him like a brother," Holly said. "I won't allow you to use him."

Jacey smiled wryly. "Do you really think Derrick would let anyone take advantage of him?"

Holly relaxed slightly. "No."

"I know we've only known each other a short time, and I really have nothing to offer him, but I love him. I'll protect him the best way I know how, even from me, if necessary."

Holly sighed but nodded. "You seem pretty nice. But hurt him, and I'll hurt you, understand?"

Jacey nodded, knowing she'd do no less for a brother she loved.

As the women walked back inside, they heard voices from the front part of the house.

"That's Ava, Roarke, and Sam." Holly walked swiftly toward the voices. Jacey followed more slowly.

These were close friends of Derrick's, and she owed it to him to get to know them, but Jacey was wary of others.

She knew the three of them were in a relationship together. Sam and Ava were both submissives. Roarke was their Dom. She'd been a bit shocked. But it wasn't like she hadn't read a few ménage romances. All purchased in secret, of course. Her parents and Stephan wouldn't have approved of her reading material.

She believed everyone should be free to live their life as they wished so long as they weren't hurting anyone else. As long as Roarke wasn't abusing his two submissives, then she had no right to judge their unusual relationship.

She stood back a bit while everyone greeted each other.

"Holly, it's great to see you!" A gorgeous man, with white-blond hair and amazingly blue eyes, took Holly into his arms, giving her a huge hug.

"How are you, Holly?" A dark-haired man asked in a deep voice, pulling Holly from the blond man's embrace. The blond man placed his arm around the tiny woman standing next to him.

"Hey Roarke," Holly greeted him with a smile.

He looked down at Holly, running a finger down her cheek. "You look pale. Are you feeling all right?" Without waiting for an answer, he raised his head and looked over at Brax. "Is she okay? Is she getting plenty of rest?"

"Sheesh, Roarke, you're as bad as these two. Don't go giving Brax any more ammunition. He's already trying to put me to bed every two minutes. I'm perfectly fine."

"Has the morning sickness stopped?" Ava asked, placing her hand on Holly's arm with concern.

Holly blew out a breath. "I wish it was just morning sickness. It goes on all day. But at least I seem to have stopped throwing up. How about you, Jacey? Please tell me the morning sickness gets better as you get further along."

Everyone's attention turned to her and Jacey resisted the urge to run and hide.

"I was actually pretty lucky," she replied. "I only had a few weeks of feeling sick."

"I think dinner is nearly ready," Derrick interjected. "Why don't we move into the dining room and I'll make the necessary introductions."

The dining room was rather grand with a large, oak table dominating the space. Beautiful artworks adorned the walls, and an amazing chandelier hung over the table.

Derrick held out the chair to his right and helped her sit.

"Roarke, Sam, and Ava, this is Jacey. Jacey, next to you is Roarke." The dark-haired man nodded to her. "Beside him is Ava." The petite woman sent her a friendly smile. "And last, but not least, is Sam."

"Hiya, sweetheart," Sam said. "So you're preggers as well?"

"Sam!" Ava scolded, whacking his arm. "I'm sorry, Jacey. You get used to him after a while."

"He grows on you," Roarke commented.

"Like an annoying kid brother you can't get rid of," Holly added.

"My heart is breaking," Sam said playfully, placing a hand over his heart as he slumped in his chair. "See the abuse I have to put up with, Jacey? I don't know why I'm friends with these people."

"Because no one else would have you," Holly told him with a grin.

Everyone chuckled as Sam shook his head, a wounded look on his face. Just like that, the ice was broken, and the conversation continued. Jacey soon found herself relaxing.

After dinner, the men wandered outside to have a cigar while the women moved into the living room.

"So are you and Brax in the city for long, Holly?" Ava asked as they all sat.

Holly shook her head. "We have to go back Sunday night. We mainly came to see Derrick. Brax and I have some things to do tomorrow. I also need to do a bit of shopping. My boobs are spilling out of all my bras, and I need some bigger clothes." She sighed.

So did Jacey. She'd taken to wearing Derrick's t-shirts because they were loose and comfortable, but her jeans were getting tight and uncomfortable.

"I'll come with you and help. We can make a girls day of it. Jacey, you'll come too, won't you?"

"Umm, well, I'm not sure. Derrick might—"

"Oh, Derrick won't mind if you come along with us," Ava said with a wave of her hand. "I'll have Roarke's driver, Max, take us. That way the men can't complain about the two of you wearing yourselves out. I'll book us in for massages, manicures, and facials. It will be great."

"Can you get us appointments at such short notice?" Jacey asked.

"Oh, no problem, I'll get Sam to book us. He can charm anyone into anything."

Of that Jacey had no doubt.

Ava clapped her hands. "It's settled then. I'll pick you both up at ten. This is going to be fun."

"So long as I don't puke up all over the masseuse's feet," Holly said dryly.

"Well, that went well." Derrick pulled the blankets back from the bed.

"Your friends are really nice." She actually meant it. She'd been surprised by how much she'd enjoyed herself in their company.

"Did you get on all right with Holly and Ava?" he asked as he climbed into the bed. Jacey lay down next to him. "I know Holly can be protective of me. I'll have a chat with her if she's giving you a hard time."

"No," she said quickly. "We talked, it's okay. I understand why she feels like she does. Besides, I think we're okay. Actually, Ava and Holly asked me to go shopping with them on Saturday."

Well, Ava had asked, but Holly hadn't seemed to hate the idea. Jacey didn't really have friends. She'd grown apart from the few when she was a child, but they'd drifted apart, and she was a bit jealous of the close relationship between Derrick and his friends.

"Of course, I have to say no. I'll think of an excuse tomorrow."

"Why would you have to say no?" He rolled onto his side and leaned up on one elbow so he could stare down at her.

"Ah, well, I'd just be intruding," she said, feeling at a distinct disadvantage with him looming over her.

"Jacey," he warned.

She sighed. "Must you know my every thought?"

"No. But the one's that upset or worry you are something I'd like to know about."

She glanced away, feeling frustrated with him. He was a hypocrite, always insisting that she talk about what she was feeling or thinking, but never giving her an insight into his thoughts.

"Jacey?"

"Derrick, you keep insisting that I talk to you, but you've totally shut down on me."

"What are you talking about?"

"You've been acting differently since our argument the other day. It's like there's this gap between us and I can't cross it. Even when we make love, it's not the same."

He sighed and pulled her close, lying on his back with her head against his chest. "I'm sorry, you're right. Hard as it is for me to admit this, I'm hurt by the fact that you think I can't protect you."

"Derrick, that's not it at all." Tears of frustration welled in her eyes, and she buried her face against him. "I just...I can't..."

"Shh." He grabbed the back of her neck, squeezing it gently.

"I know you'll protect us. But I can't risk it. I can't risk you, Derrick."

"It's okay, baby. I know. Calm down. You're supposed to stay calm and relaxed for the baby."

She snorted. "Like that's possible."

"I know this is hard for you and I haven't been making it any easier. I will stop pressuring you about your ex."

"Thank you."

"You know, I think a day out with the girls will do you a world of good."

"They want to go for massages and things, though, and I..." she trailed off.

"You don't like massages?"

"It's not that. It's just they're expensive, and I really shouldn't use my money on frivolous things."

Derrick sighed. "Didn't I give you a credit card the other day?"

He had. She hadn't wanted to take it, but he'd insisted.

"That's for emergencies."

"No, it's not. It's for you to spend."

"I don't want to take advantage of you. Holly is already half convinced I'm with you for your money. What would happen if she found out–hmm-mmm," she murmured as his mouth took hers.

"Enough," he told her in a low voice. "Holly doesn't run my life. If I hear one more word about you not using my money I'm going to take you over my knee."

"But it's just not right for me to spend your–Derrick!" she squealed, as he sat and pulled her over his lap.

"I warned you, Jacey." He shoved her nightie up.

"Derrick, let me go."

He drew her panties down her legs.

"Are you scared?" he asked.

"No. But this is crazy. You need to listen to me."

"I have listened to you. You're the one not listening to me."

He adjusted her over his knee, so her body was resting on the mattress.

"Are you uncomfortable?"

"Yes, I'm uncomfortable!" *Duh.* "You have me over your knee with my bare ass waving in the wind."

"There's no wind in here, and your ass is definitely not waving around." His voice sounded amused.

"I thought you weren't going to spank me until I said I was ready."

"You're ready, though, aren't you, Jacey? Besides, you can end this by telling me that you're going to stop putting up a fuss about using my money. I want you to go on Saturday, have a good time and spend as much money as you desire."

"No!"

Smack!

Ow, that stung. Her right butt cheek immediately flamed.

Smack! Smack! Smack!

He alternated between cheeks until her bottom burned.

"Ready to change your mind?" he asked her, rubbing the heat into her skin and the heat he'd created started to spread throughout her body. Shockingly, her clit started to throb.

"No," she gritted out.

"Very well."

He pushed her legs apart, smacking his hand down on the inside of each thigh. Jacey let out a low moan. He briskly smacked the top of each thigh four times before moving his hand lower and cupping her mound.

"Why, baby, you're wet," he said in a low voice, using his fingers to part her labia he thrust his middle finger deep inside her.

"Oh, oh," she cried out, thrusting her hips up.

"Did I tell you that you could move?" he asked. "That's going to cost you." He withdrew his finger to smack his hand down on her bottom again. "Naughty girl."

"I'm sorry!" she cried out. "Please, Derrick."

"Please what?" he asked.

"Touch me. Touch my clit. Make me come."

He paused to rub her butt cheeks again. "I haven't heard what I need to stop this, yet."

Jacey groaned. "Fine, you win. I'll spend your money. You might regret saying that, though."

He chuckled. "I trust you. I worked long and hard to build up enough money to take care of my family, to keep them safe and now you are refusing all I have to offer you."

She couldn't believe he thought that.

"Derrick, that's not true. I don't care about your money. I care about you. I want you."

"I am the type of person who needs to be needed, Jacey. I need to know that you'll turn to me for what you need. For protection, for safety, for everything."

Tears welled in her eyes. "I do know that. I just need to protect you as well."

He snorted. "You don't need to worry about me, beautiful. I plan on being around for a very long time and for many more spankings to come."

"Derrick!" Jacey tried to sit up, but he held her down.

"Did I say you could move?" His voice held a disapproving note, and she immediately lay back down.

"Seems that you need a small lesson in obedience. I'm going to play a bit, and you're going to lie very still. You may not talk. Place your arms out in front of you. That's right. Bring your legs up so you're on your knees and the pressure is off your stomach. Excellent. I expect you to keep that position. Remember what I said, no talking and lie still. Else the next spanking you get might not be quite so fun."

Jacey let out a whimper but stayed where she was. She knew he wouldn't truly harm her. But he sure could sound menacing when he wanted to.

He ran his hand down her back. "What's your safe word, Jacey?"

She remained quiet.

"That wasn't a trick question, baby. If I ask you a direct question, you can speak."

"Oh, umm, pink."

"If at any time you feel uncomfortable or scared or you just want a break from anything I expect you to say your safe word, understand? Safe words aren't just about pain."

"Yes, Sir," she said.

"Part your legs for me, beautiful."

Jacey moved her knees farther apart. Derrick slid out from under her, kneeling beside her instead. He ran his hand down the slit of her buttocks before pressing his thumb against her asshole.

Jacey bit back her protest.

He dropped his fingers down to her pussy, running them through her slick lips.

"I love how wet you are. Nothing turns me on more than knowing how aroused you get when I touch you. Now, remember what I said about remaining still."

He moved to the side of the bed, and she heard a drawer open. They'd both been tested and came back clean, so he wasn't searching for a condom. What was he doing? There was a soft squirting then he pushed her butt cheeks apart. Jacey clenched.

"Are you using your safe word, Jacey?" he asked.

"No, Sir," she replied.

"Then relax for me, beautiful. I'm just going to play a little. I promise there won't be any pain."

Jacey forced herself to relax. He rewarded her with a soft kiss on each butt cheek. He placed a dab of lube on her asshole.

"Just relax. Let me in." He pushed one finger into her tight hole as Jacey concentrated on keeping herself as relaxed as possible. He pressed his finger past the tight muscle of her sphincter until it was fully lodged inside her.

"That wasn't so bad, was it?"

Easy for him to say, he wasn't the one with a finger lodged in his butt.

"I think your good behavior deserves a little reward."

As Derrick drove his finger in and out of her asshole, he moved his free hand down to her mound. He pinched her clit lightly between his fingers then rubbed it with the tip of his middle finger.

Jacey groaned, her whole body shaking as she fought to stay in place.

Her breath coming faster, Jacey felt her whole body coil, growing tighter and tighter.

"Come for me, baby. Come on, let go now."

With a low scream, Jacey came, her asshole clenching down on his thick finger as she shook.

The bed moved as Derrick repositioned himself. Somehow he managed to keep his finger in her ass as he thrust his cock into her pussy. She whimpered at the feel of him filling her up. Having him inside her without a condom was a whole different experience. He returned his finger to her clit, flicking it steadily and Jacey knew it wasn't going to take much for her to come again.

"Christ, you feel so good. As soon as I feel your silken passage surrounding me, I want to blow my load like a randy teenager. When I come, I want you with me."

She grinned at that, clenching her passage around him.

"Damn it," he cried as he drove into her twice more then came. As he did, he lightly pinched her clit and Jacey flew over the edge, losing all of her sanity as she shook and moaned with delight.

Ten minutes later, after they'd cleaned themselves up, Jacey lay on her side, groaning as Derrick suckled on her nipples.

"Hmm, I think I've found my new favorite sleeping position," he told her.

"You can't sleep like this," she protested.

"I guess you're right. Put your leg up on my hip," he demanded. She raised her leg up, and he thrust two fingers into her pussy.

"Ahh, now I can sleep like this." He went back to sucking on her nipple.

"Derrick! I can't sleep like this." *Had he gone insane?*

He circled her clit with his thumb as the tips of his fingers flicked that special spot inside her.

"Derrick, no!" she cried, stilling when he growled at her. He pulled his hand from her pussy to give her two sharp pops on her ass.

"Stay still."

Her ass was still tender from his earlier play, and those two pops had just reignited the heat. So she made no complaints as he returned his fingers to her wet passage. He flicked her clit steadily, his tongue lapping at each nipple in turns.

Her orgasm built slowly, languidly. But as momentum grew, her pulse rate sped up, and she let out a long, low cry of need.

"Derrick, oh God."

Release washed over her, long and slow waves that made her smile with delight. Just when she thought it was ending, another wave would hit her, by the time it finished, she was exhausted and panting.

"Now, you can sleep," he told her. He cupped her mound, his fingers still buried inside her as his mouth found her nipple once more.

Jacey sighed and closed her eyes. Surprisingly, she slept deeply the whole night.

14

Jacey felt like a new woman as she stepped out of the spa. For the first time in months, she was almost completely relaxed.

"Oh my God, I feel amazing," Holly said. "And I didn't even puke on the manicurist."

Ava giggled and put her arms around the other women's waists. "Well, that is definitely something to celebrate. What say we go grab lunch and some virgin cocktails and then we can hit the shops?"

"Whatever you say," Jacey said. "I can't think, my brain is mush..."

"I'm with you there," Holly said as they walked over to where Ava's driver, Max was waiting for them patiently.

As they drove off, Ava's phone beeped.

"It'll be Roarke," she said as she dug it out of her handbag.

"Checking up on you?" Holly asked as she reached for her phone when it beeped.

"Yep," Ava replied with a giggle. "Is that Brax?"

"Yep. What trouble do they think we're going to get in to at a spa?"

"Last time we went out we ended up in a bar brawl."

"That was different," Holly said. "I wasn't pregnant then."

Jacey smiled at their words, wishing she had such a close friend.

It was a silly thought, but she couldn't help but feel a bit jealous that Derrick wasn't checking up on her.

Just then her phone beeped, and she pulled it out of her pocket to see a message from Derrick.

Everything ok?

All good. *On way 2 lunch*

B good.

She grinned.

"Derrick?" Holly asked as Jacey put her phone back in her pocket.

Jacey nodded. "He's a bit overprotective."

"Honey, all these Doms are," Ava replied. "It's in their genes or something they learn at Dom school."

"Dom school?" Jacey asked with a giggle.

"Where all Doms go to learn how to beat on a sub's ass," Holly replied wryly.

"Thank God I have Sam to run interference else Roarke would be unimaginable."

Roarke did seem pretty formidable.

"Anyway, Roarke said that he's invited all of you over for dinner tonight. The men will all meet us there after we've finished shopping. They're going to watch some game or something."

"Poor Sam," Holly said.

Ava nodded. "Sam isn't really into sports, but he has to pretend he is or he's scared he'll lose his man card."

Jacey grinned.

Exhausted, but happy, Jacey leaned her head back against the headrest of Ava's town car as Max drove them to Roarke, Sam and Ava's house, out in the suburbs.

The other girls were quiet as well, all of them tired from a long day of shopping, laughing and general silliness. It had been one of the best days of her life.

The scenery around them changed, the houses becoming larger and further apart.

"Almost home," Ava said just as light blasted through the rear window.

"What is this guy behind us doing?" Holly asked, turning around to look. "Why doesn't he pass us if he's in such a hu–" her words ended on a scream as the car rear-ended them.

"What the hell!" Ava screamed.

"He's coming again," Holly yelled, trying to reach for her handbag. She managed to grab it just as the car behind them hit them again, sending her handbag flying as the women screamed and braced themselves.

"Hold on, ladies. I don't think I can outrun him, but I'm going to try," Max called back calmly.

"Damn it, I can't reach my phone. We need to call the guys!" Holly yelled.

Jacey dug out her phone, her hand shaking as she hit Derrick's name in her contact list. He was the only name on the list. She managed to press call just as the car hit them again, sending their car flying.

It spun across the road before rolling into a ditch.

Derrick pulled out his phone, smiling as he saw Jacey's name appear on the screen.

"Hello, beautiful," he greeted her.

He froze as he heard a screeching noise then screaming.

Then nothing.

"Jacey!" he yelled. "Jacey, answer me."

The other men looked over at him in alarm, Roarke quickly switching off the television.

He hung up then tried calling her.

Nothing.

"Fuck!" He stood. "Something's happened. Jacey called, and I heard some crashing noises then screaming."

The men immediately stood, faces pale as they reached for their own phones. They raced out of the house, jamming themselves into two cars.

He had no idea where the girls were, he only knew he had to get to them quickly.

∼

Jacey opened her eyes with a groan. Shoot, her body hurt. What the hell happened? She looked around carefully, where was she?

Somebody moaned beside her. She turned to her right, whimpering as her head screamed in pain at the movement.

"What happened? Oh God, were we in an accident?"

She knew that voice. Holly. They'd been driving when a car had hit them. Jacey lowered her hand to her stomach. The baby!

"Ava!" she called out. The only light piercing the darkness was coming from their headlights.

Suddenly, she heard the sound of a car approaching.

"Did that sound like a car?" Holly asked. "Hey, help! Help!"

A queasy feeling hit her stomach, and even as her body screamed in pain, Jacey reached over to Holly, placing her hand over Holly's mouth.

"Shh, it could be the driver coming back."

She felt Holly stiffen. Shaking, Jacey drew back, frantically trying to undo her seatbelt.

The other car stopped, but there were no more sounds. Jacey strained, trying to hear anything. If they were good Samaritans stopping to help then why was it so quiet? Her suspicions grew.

What was she going to do? She had no way of protecting them.

"Holly, can you see Ava?" she whispered. Maybe if she could get the other two women to hide, then she'd be able to save them.

"What's happening?" Holly whispered back. "Oh God, Jacey, the babies. What if our babies have been hurt?"

"Holly, shh, it's going to be fine. You just need to stay calm. The baby can sense when you're upset. Just stay calm. Get down if you can and stay down."

There was the sound of a car door slamming shut. Shit, he was coming.

"Holly, act dead. Don't move. Okay?"

Just as Jacey figured the guy must be getting close, she heard another car approach. She held her breath. Then there was the sound of running and a car starting up.

Oh, God. Oh, God. He was leaving.

As she sat back in relief, pain washed over her. Dark spots danced in front of her eyes.

"What happened?" a weak voice asked.

"Ava!" Both women said with relief.

"Where am I? What's going on?"

"Ava, we've been in a car crash," Jacey said, ignoring her own pain. "Just stay calm. The guys will find us. I managed to call Derrick before we crashed."

At least she hoped she had. The other car grew closer, and she nearly cried in relief as it slowed and came to a stop.

"Roarke has GPS on the car and my phone," Ava told them. "He'll find us."

"Jacey! Holly! Ava!"

She sighed in relief as she heard Derrick's voice.

∽

DERRICK PACED up and down the hospital waiting room. He was spending far too much time in hospitals lately. What was going on? Why the hell wouldn't anyone tell them anything?

He glanced over at Brax who stood leaning against the wall, his shoulders slumped, his gaze on his feet.

Sam rested his head on Roarke's shoulder. Their fear was plain to see in the hard lines of Roarke's face and Sam's utter silence. They'd managed to locate the women quickly with the help of the GPS Roarke had in his town car. Apparently, all his vehicles had it.

Derrick made a mental note to do the same. No way could he put up with the terror of knowing something had happened to Jacey, but having no idea of where to look.

Not that she would be leaving his line of sight for the next, oh, fifty years or so.

All of the men looked up as a doctor entered the room. He seemed a bit taken aback by the tense looks sent his way, but like a true professional, he soon rallied.

"Brax Jamieson?"

Brax stepped forward. "That's me. Is Holly all right? What about the baby?"

Derrick stepped up beside him, his stomach clenched into a knot of worry for his sister-in-law and unborn niece or nephew.

"Ahh, perhaps you'd like to come with me, and we can speak in private?"

Brax shook his head. "They're family. You can speak in front of them."

"Is Holly going to be all right?" Derrick asked.

"Mrs. Jamieson has some bad bruising, we're monitoring her and the baby closely. The baby appears to be fine, but we'd like to keep her overnight as a precaution."

"Thank God," Brax breathed. "Can I see her?"

"Yes. The best thing you can do at the moment is to keep her calm. The baby and Mrs. Jamieson need reassurance that they are safe and well."

Brax nodded, taking in every word.

"What about Ava and Jacey?" Derrick asked.

Roarke and Sam came to stand up beside them. The doctor looked down at a file. "Ava Landon? You're Roarke Landon?"

He looked at Derrick.

"She's mine. I'm Roarke."

The doctor looked over at Roarke who had his arm around Sam. "Right, well, Mrs. Landon has a concussion and a sprained wrist. She's shaken, and we'll keep her overnight for observation as well."

Roarke let out a deep breath.

"Thank you, doctor!" Sam said, swinging his arms around the doctor and lifting him into the air.

The doctor looked shocked, and a little shaky as Sam let him go again.

"I'll get a nurse to show you to their rooms when they are moved out of the E.R."

"Wait. What about Jacey?" Derrick said as the doctor turned away. "Jacey Reynolds."

"The other young lady who was brought in is being treated by a colleague. He'll be along shortly."

Derrick ground his teeth in frustration, but there wasn't a lot he could do as the doctor left. A nurse soon arrived to show the others to Holly and Ava's rooms.

"Go," he told them as they looked over at him. "Don't wait around for me."

"I'll come back to check on you," Brax said.

He nodded. "Tell Holly I'll be in as soon as I can."

Derrick paced the room until a female doctor entered the room.

"Derrick Ashdown?" she asked.

"Yes. Jacey, is she all right?"

"She's got some bruising, and the baby was in a bit of distress when she arrived. We've managed to calm Ms. Reynolds down, but we're going to need to keep a close eye on her for a few days."

"Of course, whatever you think is best. Is the baby going to be all right?"

Up until now, his main focus had always been Jacey, but now with a potential risk to the baby, he found himself nearly panicking. What if something happened to the baby and there was nothing he could do?

"We're doing all that we can," the doctor told him, which wasn't all that reassuring. "The best thing is to keep Ms. Reynolds as calm as possible, she's still quite upset."

"I can do that," he said. "Can I see her?"

The doctor nodded. "Come with me."

As Derrick walked through the doorway into Jacey's room, he started breathing again.

"Hey, beautiful," he said quietly as he sat down in the chair next to her bed.

She turned her head, opening her eyes. The bruises marring her forehead stood out starkly against gray-white skin.

"Derrick." She held out her right hand, and he noticed an IV line attached. He gently clasped it tightly in his. "Derrick, I'm so scared. There was some bleeding, the baby—"

"The baby is going to be fine and so are you. I will allow nothing less."

She smiled, even as a tear dripped down her cheek. "You're so arrogant."

"It's not arrogance when I'm always right. That is something you should have learnt by now."

She snorted. "I don't think so. I've got to stop your ego from growing any bigger."

He raised a brow, staring down at her with mock sternness. "Now, see here, young lady, any more sass from you and you're going to end up over my knee, with my hand turning your ass bright red."

There was a small gasp, and Derrick turned to see a blushing young nurse standing behind them by the doorway.

"Umm, I just need to take Ms. Reynolds vitals."

Derrick watched as the nurse took Jacey's blood pressure and temperature. She fumbled around, sending him nervous glances every so often. Derrick worked hard to keep his face friendly and non-threatening. It didn't help that Jacey was biting her lip, trying to prevent herself from laughing. She let out a giggle as the poor girl left. With a groan, she raised her right hand to cover her ribs.

"You shouldn't make me laugh," she scolded.

"Me?" he said innocently. "I didn't do anything."

"That poor girl, she now thinks you're a pervert."

"You love my perverted ways."

Jacey reached back down to grab his hand, her face growing serious. "I'm so scared. I can't lose this baby, Derrick."

"You won't," he told her fiercely. "You are going to do everything the doctor tells you. Both you and the baby are going to be fine. You will remain calm and positive and allow me to look after you both."

"So bossy." But there was a flicker of a smile on her face as she scolded him. "What would I do without you, Derrick?"

"You never have to find out. You'll never be without me again. I want you to relax, baby. Let me worry about everything. You just stay calm and look after yourself and the little one."

She sighed, relaxing back into the bed. Her eyes drifted shut as he ran his fingers through her hair.

"How did you know to come looking for us?" she asked suddenly.

"I got your phone call," he told her. "Roarke had GPS on the car you were using. Bloody good idea."

She opened her eyes to stare at him suspiciously. "You're going to put it on all your cars, aren't you?"

"You bet."

"Don't you think that's overreacting?"

"I'll do whatever is needed to keep you safe." He meant every word. "I was so scared. What happened? Did a deer run out in front of you or something?"

"No," she replied. "Someone tried to run us off the road. It wasn't an accident. It was deliberate."

15

Derrick lay back on the surprisingly comfortable reclining chair in the room and looked up at the hospital ceiling.

He ran his hand through his hair, Jacey's words spinning through his mind. She'd told him everything she could remember about the crash. Someone had tried to run the girls off the road. Then they'd come back to finish the job. If that other car hadn't come along... he swallowed.

He could have lost her. Could have lost the baby. Holly. Ava.

Christ. Why would someone try to hurt them?

Jacey knew. He could tell by the haunted look on her face. Did this have something to do with her husband? He clenched his hands.

He would have questioned her further, but a different nurse had entered the room, telling him that Jacey had to rest. He could see the exhaustion on her face and knew that the best thing she could do right now was get some sleep.

So as Jacey slept, Derrick lay back on the chair the nurse had found for him and stared at the ceiling, worrying. There had been no way he was leaving her. No way in hell. In the morning he'd arrange for round the clock security for all the women. He'd also question

Roarke about his driver, who had been released from the hospital with a mild concussion and bruising.

Derrick wondered how long Jacey needed to stay in the hospital. He wouldn't go against doctor's orders, but if someone were trying to harm her, then the best place he could protect her was at his house.

What if it wasn't about Jacey?

He knew that Roarke, Sam, and Brax were staying with Ava and Holly for the night. The women would be protected tonight. Tomorrow he would find out exactly what was going on.

∼

Jacey woke up disorientated and in pain. She blinked, looking around. White on white on white. The smell of disinfectant hit her nose as well as the noise of people moving around and talking.

Hospital. Accident. The baby.

She reached down to cover her stomach.

"Jacey? Hey, you're awake." Derrick looked down at her, a smile on his tired face. His hair was sticking out at all angles, looking more rumpled than she'd ever seen him. In fact, she didn't think she'd ever seen him with a wrinkle in his clothes. He always managed to look like he'd just stepped out of a fashion magazine.

"Derrick, the baby? Is it okay?"

"The doctor will be in soon," he reassured her. "They're going to do an ultrasound and check on the baby."

"Okay, okay, that's good. Derrick," she grabbed his hand, staring up at him urgently. "There are things I need to tell you, things I should have told you before, but I thought I was protecting you. He's found me. He's coming after me."

"Jacey, shh, I know we need to talk and we will." He gave her a stern look. "But I want you to remain calm right now. Once the doctor's been in, I'm going to go and check in with the others. I've arranged for security, they'll be here within the hour. I don't want you worrying, understand?"

"Holly, Ava, are they okay? Holly's baby?"

"They're fine. In fact, they're probably going home today. Ava had a bit of a concussion, and they wanted to keep an eye on Holly's baby, but everything looks to be okay."

"Thank God." She relaxed back on the bed, some of the tension leaving her face. "I would never forgive myself if something happened to them. It was my worst nightmare. I was so scared something would happen to you, that I never considered anyone else. We all could have died." Tears welled in her eyes.

Derrick cupped her cheeks between his palms. "Baby, it's going to be all right. I promise. I'll make sure of it."

∼

DERRICK KNOCKED on Holly's hospital room door before opening it and stepping inside. Brax glanced up, his face tired and lined with stress.

"Derrick," Holly said with a smile. She was pale, but her eyes lit up when she saw him.

"Hey, love, how are you feeling?"

"I'm fine."

She attempted to sit up, and Brax immediately jumped to his feet, holding her shoulders down.

"Lie down, Holly."

"Brax, I'm tired of lying down. I need to move around. The doctor said I'm fine, now let me up."

Brax growled under his breath, but relented and handed her the controls for the bed.

"What exactly did the doctor say?" Derrick asked, sitting on a chair and grabbing hold of her hand.

Holly shrugged. "Nothing much."

"She's bruised, and she needs to take it easy for a while. Lots of bed rest and nothing stressful," Brax told him.

"The baby?" Derrick asked.

"We saw him or her on the ultrasound," Holly said excitedly. "It was amazing. I was shocked by how clear it was."

Derrick grinned. "It is pretty amazing, isn't it? They just did another ultrasound on Jacey, and it's something I'll never get tired of seeing." It had been a great relief to see the baby dancing around inside her.

"How is Jacey? And Ava? Brax won't let me get up and visit them."

"The doctor said you're to rest," Brax told her.

"The doctor also said I could go home," Holly told him sternly. "Stop being such a fussy old man."

"Honey, you're just racking up the punishments."

Holly waved him away. "You won't punish me while I'm recovering from an accident and pregnant."

"No, but I'm keeping a little notebook with all your transgressions. Once this baby is born and you're fully recovered, you and I are going to have a day of reckoning."

"Just a day?" Derrick asked dryly as Holly gulped.

"You know, you're not supposed to upset me," Holly accused.

Brax immediately grew pale. "Christ, I'm sorry, Holly. Are you okay? Any cramps?"

"That was mean," Derrick scolded Holly.

She sighed, looking guilty. "You're right. Brax, I'm sorry, I never should have said that. I feel fine. I promise."

"You're right, though, I'm supposed to be keeping you calm."

"And you are. I'm just being a brat." She grabbed his hand, squeezing it. Then she turned to Derrick.

"So Jacey and the baby are okay?"

"Jacey has some bruising. They want to keep her in another day since she had some bleeding. I've just seen Ava, she's had the all-clear to go home. They're waiting on the discharge papers."

"Thank God."

Brax frowned. "In your text last night, you said they might have been deliberately run off the road?"

"From what Jacey told me, yes, I believe so."

"That's what I think too," Holly agreed. "No way was it an accident. He just kept coming at us, Max couldn't get away. Then after the crash, I heard a car stop, but no one called out. I wasn't really sure what was going on, but Jacey was really suspicious when nobody came running to help us. Whoever it was quickly took off when another car started to approach. Who would want to hurt us, though? It was Roarke's car, was this aimed at him?"

"Good guess, love, but Derrick's pretty sure they were after Jacey."

"Jacey, why?" Brax asked.

"Jacey's husband abused her. She left him a few months ago, and she's been hiding from him ever since. She thinks he wants to kill her. I need to get all the details from her, but I'm also worried about upsetting her too much. This needs to be done delicately when she feels safe and secure."

Brax nodded.

"How horrible," Holly said, looking at him shocked. "I just can't imagine anyone abusing Jacey. She's so fragile and sweet. I admit, at first I was a bit taken aback by how quickly you'd moved her into your house and I kind of thought she might be a gold-digger, but after spending the day with her, I realized she's kind of shy. She's so sweet and lovely. That bastard."

Derrick nodded in agreement. "Anyway, I wanted to warn you guys to be on the alert. If it is Jacey's ex, I don't think he'll come after any of you. But in case we're wrong about any of this, I'd be much happier if you accepted some extra security."

"Security?" Brax asked.

"I've spoken to Roarke, he's got a good security system, but he's going to hire some men to watch the house. I'd like to do the same for you guys. Let me hire a few men to watch over your place."

"Derrick, don't you think you're overreacting, I mean, you should be worried about Jacey's security, not ours," Holly said.

"Oh, believe me, her security is very much on my mind. But the two of you are my family. I need to make sure you're protected."

Brax was silent for a long moment. Derrick wasn't sure if he would take him up on his offer. It had taken a lot of talking before Brax allowed him to buy Holly a new car. Brax was a proud man, and he made a good living with his construction business, but he didn't have the money to pay for round-the-clock security. Derrick just hoped he'd push past his pride and see that this was for the best.

"All right. But only if you promise to keep us updated and for God's sake, be careful."

Derrick nodded with relief. "Don't worry. I intend to ensure that I live a long and healthy life."

∽

JACEY LOOKED around Derrick's bedroom as he placed her gently on the bed. "I never thought I'd be so pleased to be back in this bed." She stuck out her lower lip. "Though I'm getting really tired of resting. Couldn't I just sit on the sofa in the living room? I promise not to move around."

Derrick shook his head. "Sorry, baby. The doctor said you were to have a few more days of bed rest then you can slowly resume your normal activities."

"Like I even know what normal is anymore," she muttered as he stripped off her clothes and helped her dress in one of his shirts.

"I know, beautiful. But one day we'll get there. One day we'll be so normal you'll almost wish for a bit of excitement."

She snorted. "I've had enough excitement to last me a lifetime, thank you very much."

He sat beside her, gently pushing her hair back from her face. "When I think of how close I came to losing you and the little one…" his voice trailed off, actually cracking with his emotion.

"But you didn't." She grabbed hold of his hand, placing it on her belly. "We're fine. The doctor said so."

"And I'm going to make sure you stay that way."

Jacey sighed. "It's time to tell you everything, isn't it?"

"Yes."

She leaned back against the pillows he'd put behind her. "If I'd had the courage, I would have left Stephan long before I did. When he first started abusing me, I should have packed up my bags and taken off."

"Why didn't you?"

"Because I thought that for once I was doing the right thing by staying married to him. All my life I'd been a failure, a mistake. I was born the wrong sex, I wrecked my mother's body so she couldn't have other children, denying my parents the boy they'd always wanted."

"Baby, you can't know that."

"Oh, but I do," she said matter-of-factly. "Because they told me."

Derrick clenched his hands against the anger rising through him. How could her parents have done that? Parents should protect and look after their children, love and guide them. Not destroy their self-esteem.

"When did they tell you this?"

"When I was eight years old and pestering them for a puppy," she said. "My mother turned to me, told me that I was never getting a dog so I should stop asking. She said I should be thankful to get a roof over my head and food on my plate, and that the only reason they kept me around was for appearances. I wasn't wanted, wasn't loved and I wouldn't ever get anything I asked for."

Derrick felt like murdering the old bitch.

"I don't think I ever asked for anything again." She glanced at him. "Oh, it wasn't all bad. I received a fantastic education. I was sent to the best schools, I had ballet lessons and riding lessons, and despite her words, I never went hungry or without anything."

Except for love, affection, acceptance.

"I tried to make them notice me with good grades, by doing everything they asked. Somehow it was never enough. Then one day, when I was home from College, my father brought home a young colleague of his. My father is a partner in a prestigious law firm."

"Stephan was the young colleague?"

"Yes. Right away, he paid attention to me, he noticed me and for once my parents were pleased with me. It helped that Stephan was so charming. It was like he'd stepped right out of a romance book. He had a dominant streak, yet he could also be sensitive and caring. God, he had me fooled. I fell for him, and I actually made my parents proud the day I married him."

"Did you really fall for him or was it simply that you had your parents approval?" he asked.

She blinked, frowning. "Well, I'm not sure. A bit of both, maybe."

"When he started abusing you, did you ever consider going to your parents for help?"

She blinked back tears. "No. I knew they wouldn't help. They loved Stephan. As long as I was with him my relationship with my parents was better. Not great, but better."

"Please don't tell me that you stayed with him because of them."

"Partly, maybe. I was too scared to leave him. I knew he wouldn't let me go. I knew if I left that I would always be on the run, looking over my shoulder, afraid."

She cleared her throat, her distress easy to see.

"Baby, we can wait to do this if you're not feeling up to it."

"No," she told him, holding his hand tighter. "I need to tell you everything. It's just hard to remember. I wish I'd left then. I wish I'd had the courage. Stephan has this half-brother, Evan. We didn't see a lot of him, thank goodness. He scared me, he was always watching me with these cold eyes. I knew he didn't have much of a conscience and I could never understand why Stephan was so close to him.

"Stephan was very big on image, he was forever dictating to me about the way to act and dress in public. Honestly, you'd have thought he was royalty, the way he carried on. Evan was coarse and rude, he wears jeans and t-shirts, watches football. When he drank, he became more obnoxious. All things Stephan would never dream of doing. He wanted to promote himself as a perfect, upstanding family man. But then I found out exactly what Evan's function in Stephan's life was."

She swallowed, growing paler.

"Stephan had an assistant, Gerry. He was a nice man, well, he was always kind to me. Turns out, Gerry must have been gathering information about Stephan to blackmail him. I was supposed to be at my parents, but they'd had to suddenly go to New York, so I came home early. No one heard my return, I guess. I thought no one was home. But as I walked toward the stairs, I heard this noise. For some reason,

I didn't call out. I don't know why, but I just tiptoed to Stephan's study."

Jacey licked her lips.

"The door was partially open. Inside...inside, Gerry was on his knees, his hands and feet tied. Evan had a gun held to Gerry's head, while Stephan paced back and forth. Stephan was furious, I'd never seen him so angry. He was accusing Gerry of trying to blackmail him, of betraying him. He held a notebook in his hand. I don't know what Gerry had on him, but it must have been significant for Stephan to be so angry."

Christ. He had a bad feeling he knew where this was going. He could see her standing there, terrified, watching everything unfold.

"Gerry was crying, begging them to let him go, not to kill him. I-I wanted to do something, but it was like I was frozen, I couldn't move, I couldn't speak."

"If you'd tried, they'd have killed you."

She raised her gaze to his. "They still might," she whispered. "Gerry was trying to explain, making excuses. Stephan was nodding, as though he were actually listening. Then he grabbed a lighter and set the notebook on fire before throwing it into the fireplace. He asked Gerry if there was any more evidence. Gerry kept saying no. Evan told Stephan he was lying. Evan stepped around Gerry and kicked him in the crotch. He fell onto his side, choking and screaming. That's when I saw his face. They'd beaten him up, well, Evan must have. Stephan wouldn't have lowered himself to actually doing anything physical. Gerry's eyes were swollen, his nose looked broken."

Derrick moved so he sat beside her. Leaning against the headboard, he pulled her onto his lap, holding her tight as he rocked her. Her body was shaking.

"Evan pulled him up onto his knees and whispered something to him. Stephan crouched down and looked at Gerry, told him that he'd made a big mistake by crossing him. Then he turned away and-and Evan, he shot him. One shot, right in the head."

Her eyes were wide, her breath coming in short, shallow pants.

Derrick held her closer. "Jacey, look at me. Look at me," he demanded. Immediately, her gaze met his. "He can't hurt you." He didn't make it a question. There could be no doubt in her mind.

She nodded. Tears glistened in her eyes.

"Did they see you at the door?" he asked.

Jacey shook her head. "I thought I was screaming, but it must have been in my head because they didn't turn to look at me. I-I stepped away from the room as quietly as I could. Then I left the house, got in my car and drove off. I just drove and drove. I stopped once and got some money out of an ATM. Then I drove again. When I was so exhausted, I could barely think I checked in to a hotel under the name Jacey Reynolds and slept. When I woke up, I had to come up with a plan. I knew I had to disappear. So I sold my car and dumped my phone and all my ID."

She rubbed her forehead tiredly, and his heart ached at how alone and terrified she must have been.

"I knew it wouldn't take Stephan long to figure things out. He would send Evan on my trail. I had about a thousand dollars and no idea what I was going to do. I figured I couldn't do much without a social security number or ID, but I thought I might be able to get some sort of job, maybe rent a room. Start over. So I bought a bus ticket to Austin. I'd never been to Texas."

"You were very brave."

"I was terrified," she confessed. "I didn't know what I was going to do. I always figured that Stephan would find me eventually and kill me, but after I found out I was pregnant, I knew I had to do whatever I could to stay alive, at least until the baby was born."

"He's not going to get to either of you now."

"But Stephan can't let me live, Derrick. He must have found me. Evan was probably the one driving that car the other night. They'll kill me when they find me, and anyone who is helping me. Anyone close to me is in jeopardy."

"I'm not without my own resources. I know it must seem like Evan and Stephan are infallible, but they're not. They're just men."

She shivered. "I'm not sure they are. They have no conscience.

Evan actually smiled as he shot Gerry. He enjoyed killing him. And Stephan, he's not any better. He gets Evan to do his dirty work, but he's just as evil. They have no honor. They don't fight fair."

"Oh, baby, neither do I. Not when it comes to protecting those I love. Where I grew up, you were either a leader or a follower. I always led. I know how to fight dirty, and I know how to protect those I love. Now, tell me their names. Their full names."

"Evan Sanders and Stephan Worthington."

Derrick frowned. "Stephan Worthington, I know that name." Suddenly it hit him. "Jesus Christ, Stephan Worthington is the Illinois State Attorney General."

She nodded. "Yes, and he's planning on running for Governor. My full name is Jacinta Worthington. My father is George Peters of Peters, Reynolds, and James law firm. He's backing Stephan's campaign. What I know would ruin him. You see why he has to get rid of me?"

He'd known her husband must be someone with connections, but he hadn't realized that he'd recognize his name. Stephan Worthington was good friends with the Vice President of the United States. Shit, this would rock the State of Illinois and work its way up to Washington D.C.

But he didn't give a shit about any of that. His job was to look after Jacey and their baby.

"Don't worry, I'm not going to let him or his brother anywhere near you. No matter who he is."

16

Derrick sat back in his chair as he ended the phone call with Roarke. Jacey was upstairs sleeping. Christ, when he thought about what she'd gone through, he wanted to hunt down those two bastards himself.

But this required some more delicate manoeuvring, which is where Roarke came in. Roarke had immediately promised to contact an old friend of his who owned a security firm. Hunter Black was a former Navy SEAL, and his employees all had a military or Government background.

Roarke had assured Derrick that if anyone could keep Jacey safe and investigate Stephan Worthington, then it was Hunter and his team. They'd be here in the morning. In the meantime, Derrick knew he wouldn't get much sleep.

He stood up and paced across the room.

The more people who knew about this, the more danger Jacey would be in.

And any danger was unacceptable to him.

JACEY WALKED DOWN THE STAIRS, hearing voices coming from the living room. She didn't want to intrude on a private meeting, so she moved toward the kitchen, coming to a standstill as she saw a large man carving up some meat. Thick sandwiches were piled high on a plate beside him.

He turned to look at her, and she almost stepped back out of the room. He wasn't that tall, but he was stocky. His tight t-shirt outlined the thick muscles of his arms and shoulders. His bicep seemed larger than her thigh. A huge scar ran down the side of his face, the skin around it puckered, giving him a menacing look.

"W-who are you?" A burglar wouldn't be standing there so calmly making sandwiches.

"Friend of Roarke's."

A friend of Roarke's? Where was Derrick?

"You hungry?" he asked.

"Ahh, yes, I guess," she replied.

"Good. Pregnant. I'll make you a special sandwich."

"Umm, don't go to any trouble," she whispered, feeling like she'd turned a corner into the Twilight Zone.

He just grunted.

Jacey backed out of the room. She needed to find Derrick. Now.

She let out a screech of surprise as she backed into something hard and unyielding. She turned. Ice-blue eyes stared down at her, analyzing her. Her heart in her throat, she could only stand there, staring back.

If she were smart, she'd be running the other direction right now. But she had a feeling she wouldn't get far.

"Derrick's looking for you," the entirely too-scary man said. "Come into the living room."

He turned away as though fully expecting her to follow him. "Who are you?" she whispered.

"Hunter," he said over his shoulder as though that explained everything.

With a shake of her head, Jacey followed him down the hallway toward the living room.

"Jacey!"

She turned to find Derrick walking toward her, a look of intense relief on his face. He drew her into his arms.

"Christ, when you weren't upstairs in our room, I almost had a heart attack," he told her.

"Sorry, I woke up hungry so I thought I'd come down for something to eat."

He ran his hand over her hair. "How are you feeling?"

"Better," she told him.

"Good. Come into the living room. I want you to meet some people."

"Umm, yeah, I think I've already met a couple of them. Are you holding an annual bad-ass meeting or something?"

Derrick let out a surprised laugh. Tension drained from his body just as she'd hoped.

"I don't think I've ever heard you say the word ass before." He placed an arm over her shoulder, bringing her closer to him as he led her into the living room.

Hunter sat beside another large man who was working on a tablet. A third man sat hunched over a computer that was set up on a table in the corner of the room. He didn't bother to look up.

"She doesn't obey very well, does she?" Hunter said with disapproval, searing her with those icicle eyes.

"Depends on who's doing the ordering," she replied angrily. No way was she going to be bullied by him, no matter how scary looking he was.

Hunter raised a brow, his eyes flickering over her again as though reassessing her. "Well, you're going to have to learn how to follow my orders, and quickly, sweetheart."

She glanced up at Derrick in confusion. Who were these guys?

Derrick took her hand, leading her to the sofa across from where Hunter and the other man sat.

"Jacey, this is Hunter Black. He owns a security firm. I've hired his firm to help protect you and to investigate Stephan."

"That was fast," she said.

"I owed Roarke a favor," Hunter said.

"You're friends with Roarke?" she asked.

"I wouldn't exactly call us friends," Hunter replied.

"They're as friendly as anyone gets with Hunter," the man sitting next to Hunter said.

"This is Jaron." Hunter nodded to the dark-haired man beside him. "The guy glued to the computer is Connor, our tech expert."

Connor glanced up briefly.

"Nice to meet you both. Umm, what about the man in the kitchen?"

"That's Tiny. He'll be in shortly. I also have other men stationed outside the house."

Tiny? She didn't see what was so tiny about him.

Before she could ask any further questions, Tiny entered carrying a large platter full sandwiches.

"Here." He sat the plate down on the coffee table between the two couches. "Yours." He pointed to the top sandwich, then looked at Jacey.

"Thank you," she replied, picking up the sandwich, not daring to do anything else. She took a bite, her eyes closing at the bliss that crossed her taste buds. "Wow, this is really good."

Tiny just grunted.

"Is your business located in Austin, Mr. Black?"

"No," Hunter replied. "We're based in Dallas. We'll soon have everything we need on this guy," Hunter said to Derrick. "He'll be running scared once we're through. Won't know what hit him."

"Be careful not to underestimate him or Evan," Jacey warned, the sandwich sitting heavily in her stomach.

"Oh, don't you worry, we know all about Evan Sanders," Hunter said. "He's the other reason we took this job. We've been after him for a while."

"Really?"

"He's a psychotic bastard," Hunter told her, his eyes growing colder. "Everyone will be safer when he's gone, and I'll be a lot happier."

Somehow she couldn't quite see Hunter as ever being happy.

"Jacey, I want you to tell us everything you know about Sanders and his brother."

By the time Jacey was finished answering Hunter's questions, she felt completely drained. She leaned against Derrick's shoulder, trying to ignore the throbbing in her head.

"Headache."

She looked over at Tiny who had spoken.

"Just a small one."

Derrick turned her head gently, so she was facing him. He ran his thumb across her cheek. Then he turned to face Hunter. "I'm taking her upstairs to rest. Any more questions can wait."

Hunter narrowed his gaze but didn't say anything as Derrick stood then scooped Jacey up into his arms. He walked from the room.

"I just got out of bed," she complained as he walked into their bedroom and placed her on the bed.

"The doctor said you needed rest and little stress. This situation isn't exactly stress-free, but I can make sure you rest."

"Do you really think they can help?" she asked after he'd tucked her in.

He ran his hand over her hair. "If anyone can, it's Hunter and his team. I'd put my money on them any day."

Yeah, that's what she thought too.

"I have something for you." He stood and walked over to his nightstand. Pulling open the drawer, he drew out a jewelry box.

Her hands shook as she took it. It was too large to be a ring box. Opening it, she saw a gorgeous locket made from rose gold.

"It's beautiful."

"I want you to wear it all times, promise me."

She gazed up at him and saw the intensity in his face.

"I may not be able to marry you yet. But I can claim you. You are mine, Jacey Reynolds. I don't ever want you to forget it."

"I won't," she whispered. "I could never forget that. I never want to."

He grinned and slipped it around her neck, doing up the clasp at the back.

"All mine," he said with satisfaction.

Jacey placed her hand on his chest. "You know, you could also claim me in another way." She couldn't quite believe she was being so bold with the house filled with strangers, but she needed him desperately.

Derrick shook his head, a look of intense need on his face. "As much as I would like to take you up on that, you need to rest. Plus, I want to check with the doctor before we have sex." He placed his hand over her stomach.

"I feel fine, Derrick."

He shook his head. "I won't chance hurting you."

She liked how much care he took with her. "Okay. How are we going to get to the doctor's, though?"

"Don't worry, Hunter is formulating a plan. You just get some rest, baby girl."

He sat with her, running his hand over her head until she drifted off into sleep.

17

Jacey smoothed down the sexy, babydoll nightgown she was wearing, nervous anticipation filling her.

It had been five days since the doctor had given the go ahead to resume normal activities, and yet Derrick still hadn't touched her. Her bruises were fading and they no longer hurt. She needed to show him that she wasn't fragile, that she wasn't going to break.

Sure, there were a number of men in the house, but their bedroom was well away from the commandeered living area. She'd grown used to having the guys around; it was going to be quiet when they left.

If they ever left. It had over a week since they'd nearly been run off the road and nothing else had happened.

Hunter seemed to think that Stephan and Evan were biding their time, waiting for the right moment. Jacey just wanted this over and done with. She was starting to think that the only way to end this was to set a trap.

With her as the bait.

But she hadn't quite worked up the courage to suggest that yet.

Sighing, she sat on the side of the bed. What was she doing? She wasn't good at seduction. Even though Ava and Holly had assured her that this outfit would rock Derrick's socks off, she still wasn't sure.

She nibbled at her thumbnail. But she wanted him to touch her, to take her, hell, she'd give anything for him to threaten to spank her at the moment. He'd been treating her like a china doll, and that had to stop.

As Jaron liked to say, all you needed was a good plan, and the rest would fall into place. Jaron had turned out to be the most talkative of the bunch. Connor was pretty much attached to his computer while Tiny still spoke in one or two word sentences. Hunter spoke, but most of the time it was to tell her what to do or not to do. The man was a regular grouch.

Out of all of them, though, it was Tiny who had grown on her the most. He was constantly trying to take care of her in his gruff way, cooking her favorite foods, coaxing her into eating when she didn't think she was hungry. She was even starting to put on some weight, and the baby was becoming more pronounced, which made her so happy.

Standing, she turned from side to side in front of the large freestanding mirror.

The girls were right. She was going to knock Derrick's socks off.

～

DERRICK WALKED up the stairs to their room long after he knew Jacey would have gone to sleep. He felt slightly bad about staying out of their bed until she fell asleep and then rising before she woke. He knew she didn't understand why he hadn't made love to her since the car crash, and he hated the confusion and hurt on her face when she looked at him.

But he was simply too frightened of hurting her. He didn't know if he had it in him to be gentle right now. He was feeling too primal to go slow and easy.

If he took her, it would be hard, his walls would come crashing down, and all the dominance and fear he'd been holding back would come pouring out.

There was no way he would ever risk hurting her, so it was best that he didn't touch her at all. She would thank him in the long run. The doctor had given them the all-clear to enjoy sex, but Derrick was certain he wouldn't approve of the things Derrick wanted to do to her.

Like, tie her to the bed, spread-eagled and at his mercy. He'd then feast on her pussy, driving her over the edge into orgasm over and over until she was limp with pleasure, completely satiated. Then he'd fill her ass with a plug, driving it into her, thrusting it into her tight hole until she was begging him to take her.

But he would hold off, taking her nipples into his mouth, playing with them, toying with them until neither of them could take any more.

Then he'd take her. Over and over. Rough, hard and fast.

No. He shook his head. She was pregnant, fragile. He had no business even thinking about taking her this way. Taking a deep breath, Derrick turned the door handle and stepped into the bedroom.

Finally, Jacey thought as the door opened and Derrick walked inside. She'd almost given up on him and gone to sleep. But as she watched his eyes widen, the way he stilled and just stared at her, she was glad she'd stayed awake.

She'd propped herself up on the bed, some pillows behind her back and her legs spread out wide.

She wasn't wearing any panties.

His gaze roamed over her stiffening nipples, easily visible in the see-through teddy, down to her shaved pussy. She wished she could have waxed it, but wasn't about to ask Hunter if he could arrange that.

She could just imagine how that conversation would go.

"What are you doing?" Derrick asked, shutting the door behind him. "Anyone could have come in here and seen you."

Okay, not quite the reaction she'd been hoping for.

"Everyone else knocks," she told him.

"Where the hell did you get that?" he asked, gesturing at her teddy.

"I bought it the day I went out with Holly and Ava. Don't you like it?"

His reaction was putting a damper on her arousal, and she had to fight the urge to close her legs.

"It's not exactly going to keep you warm," he told her in a harsh voice.

That did it. Temper racing through her veins, she sat up.

"It's not supposed to keep me warm. You are. Although I suppose if you don't find me attractive anymore, I could go find someone else to keep me warm."

His eyes widened. Reaching around behind him, he locked the door.

"Oh, baby, you didn't just dare me. You don't ever want to do that."

Jacey gulped as he stalked toward her. This was more the reaction that she'd been hoping for, although now that she had his interest, she started to wonder at her sanity.

"I hope you're fully prepared for what you just started," he told her. "If not, say so now."

She swallowed heavily. Part of her wasn't so sure, but she wasn't about to back down now.

She raised her chin. "I am. Are you?"

A wicked grin crossed his face. "I need to go and get a few things. While I'm out of the room, you're going to strip yourself naked. From now on, when we're alone in this room together you'll always be naked."

Christ, what had she been thinking?

"I want you on your hands and knees at the end of the bed on your hands and knees, your legs spread nice and wide."

Derrick unlocked the door and left the room, leaving her in a slightly dazed state. Sitting up, she removed the teddy. Well, that seemed like a waste of money. Always naked in their bedroom? Was he kidding?

She was pretty sure he wasn't. Not in the slightest.

On her hands and knees, Jacey positioned herself at the edge of the bed then spread her legs wide. She blushed, realizing exactly how on show she was. Two minutes later the door opened and shut. The lock clicked into place.

"Beautiful," Derrick told her. He ran his hand over her backside, and she trembled in anticipation. "I find it extremely sexy when you obey me."

Pleasure engulfed her. She liked pleasing him. This is what she'd dreamed of having with Stephan, only that had ended in a nightmare.

"What are you thinking, Jacey?"

"Nothing much."

He smacked his hand down on her buttocks.

"What were you thinking about, Jacey? And I suggest you answer me truthfully."

She caught her breath, letting it out slowly. "I was just thinking about how much I enjoy pleasing you."

He kissed one butt cheek then the other.

"Thank you." He ran his hand between her legs, circling his finger around her clit.

He pressed on her shoulders. "Crouch right down, baby. I want this gorgeous ass sticking up."

She did as he ordered, her breath catching as he ran his hands over her still hot butt cheeks, rubbing the heat in. He parted her cheeks and leaning in, licked her asshole.

Jacey groaned the feel of his tongue against her asshole deliciously, darkly erotic. With two of his fingers, he circled her clit as he lapped at her asshole. Jacey bit her lip, trying to hold still, to keep her cries of need from escaping. But they fought their way free, filling the room as her breath came in hard, fast pants.

Her arousal grew higher, her need overwhelming... and then he pulled away.

"Derrick," she groaned in protest.

A heavy smack to her ass. "What do you call me?"

"Sir?" she replied.

"Better, much better," he said with satisfaction.

"Why did you stop, Sir?"

"Because you were about to come and tonight you have to earn your pleasure. Reach back and part your butt cheeks for me."

It was silly to feel embarrassed, he'd just had his tongue on her asshole for God's sake, but she couldn't stop the heat from rising in her cheeks as she held herself open to him, putting herself completely on display.

"Very nice," he told her. He prodded at her asshole with a lubricated finger, pushing it slowly inside her. In and out. Over and over.

Jacey fought not to move, not to thrust her hips back onto that single digit. Derrick pushed a second finger into her asshole, twisting them, pumping them in and out. He teased her throbbing clit with fingers from her other hand.

On the verge of coming, he withdrew both sets of fingers, patting her mound comfortably as she cried out at the loss.

"Shh," he told her. "Hold those cheeks wide open for me. Very good." Something thick and foreign prodded against her asshole. "Open up. Relax. I'm just plugging you. It's a bit bigger than the last one, but you can take it."

A bit bigger? He had to be kidding. Jacey took in a deep breath, letting it out slowly, forcing herself to relax as he relentlessly pushed the plug inside her.

"Damn, you look so pretty with my plug inside you." He twisted the plug, making her breath catch in arousal. "Arms out above your head. Good, keep them there."

Derrick ran his hands up her thighs, over her buttocks, pressing down on the plug, making her groan. He pressed against her back, and she felt his erection, thick and hard, against her buttocks as he reached underneath her to massage her breasts.

"You like having your breasts played with, don't you, baby? You love having your nipples suckled and pinched."

"Y-yes, Sir," she cried as he pinched first one nipple then the other. Her breasts had become far more sensitive with her pregnancy, and her clit throbbed with every touch of his fingers against her nipples.

"Don't come without permission, baby. I'd hate to have to punish you tonight when I have so much in store for you," he whispered.

Jacey whimpered, trying hard to think of anything else but his erection brushing against her buttocks, the thick plug that was settled deep into her ass, the fingers mercilessly playing with her nipples.

He pulled back then drew her up until she was kneeling, her weight resting on her haunches.

"Scoot forward a bit; I don't want you tumbling off the end of the bed. Hands on your head, very nice," he praised. "Keep those thighs nice and wide. Your pussy should always be accessible to me. In fact," he knelt in front of her and reached down to run his finger along the lips of her pussy, "I think that when we're here alone that your legs should always be open to me, even when you sleep."

He'd gone insane.

She dropped her hands to his shoulders, resting them there as she started to sway with pleasure. Immediately, he stopped, and she glanced up at him in question.

"Where are your hands supposed to be?" he growled.

Jacey snatched them away from his shoulders, placing them on her head. "Sorry, Sir."

He shook his head. "Not good enough." He sighed. "Guess I'm just going to have to bind you." He rose from the bed. "Hands behind your back."

He tied her wrists together, tugging at the binding to test them.

"Wiggle your fingers. Good. Tell me if you have any numbness or tingling," he ordered.

"Yes, Sir," she replied as he knelt on the bed in front of her.

Derrick cupped her breasts, pushing them together so he could lick her nipples. They stiffened, elongating as he pinched and suckled them in turns. Moisture coated her pussy, her breath coming faster and she knew she was close to coming.

Clenching her jaw, she fought against the impending orgasm.

"Such beautiful breasts." Derrick leaned back, holding her breasts up. "Look how red your nipples are."

She glanced down at herself. Her nipples stood at attention, begging for more pleasure as his tanned hands held her breasts up.

Derrick let her breasts drop as he ran one hand down her stomach to her pussy. He dipped two fingers into her welcoming pussy.

"Sir, please," she begged as he thrust his fingers in and out.

"Please what?"

"Please let me come."

He pulled his fingers out, and she cried out in denial as he grinned down at her.

"No, not yet." He smeared her juices all over his thick shaft. "First, I want you to lick your cream from my cock."

He untied her hands then sat back against the headboard and spread his legs wide. Jacey shuffled herself forward, leaning down she took the head of him into her mouth. She sucked on him eagerly, bobbing her head up and down.

"Aw, Christ, baby. That feels so damn good. Faster. Stronger."

Jacey increased her speed, delighting in his groans of pleasure. When he reached down and pulled her off his shaft, she moaned in protest.

"Uh, uh," he said as he lifted her, so she was straddling him. "Much as I appreciate your enthusiasm, I decide when and how I come, not you." He pinched each nipple. Hard. She arched her back, groaning.

"Now turn around. Make sure you don't lose that plug in your ass."

She turned, so she was facing away from him, still straddling his hips.

"Rise up, lower yourself on my cock very slowly."

He held his cock with one hand, his other hand wrapped around her bound wrists as she lowered herself onto his thick shaft. They both let out a low moan of pleasure once he was fully inside her.

Derrick placed his hands on her hips. "Ride me, beautiful." He guided her movements, slow at first then increasing in speed until she was slamming her hips down onto him, her pussy making suctioning sounds as she took him deep inside her.

With the plug in her ass and Derrick lodged deep in her pussy, she was overflowing, full and needy. He let go of her right hip, reaching around with one hand to flick her clit with his fingers.

"Oh, oh, oh," she cried out. There was no way she could hold back her orgasm. "Please, Sir, let me come."

"You can come, baby girl."

With a cry that she quickly tried to stifle, she came violently, shuddering around him, barely hearing his own shout of completion as he emptied himself inside her.

Jacey slumped forward, murmuring a protest as he rose with her in his arms. Carrying her into the bathroom, he sat her on the counter before turning the water on in the shower.

"That was amazing," she told him.

"Baby, that was nothing. There is plenty more to come."

Oh, sugar.

～

"Why haven't you made another move?" Stephan demanded as soon as Evan picked up the phone.

"An issue has developed," Evan said.

"An issue? What sort of fucking issue? You know, if you'd just finished her off the other night then we wouldn't have any *issues*."

"Did you want me to get caught? I guess that wouldn't worry you, though, would it? Two birds with one stone, get rid of the two witnesses to what you did."

"What I did? You're the one who shot him," Stephan yelled back.

"On your orders, brother dearest. How much have I done for you over the years and yet you're happy to throw me to the dogs."

Stephan reined in his temper, realizing this was going nowhere fast. "I'm sorry, of course, I don't want that. I'm just eager to get this taken care of, you know that. I would never let you go down for any of this. You're my brother, we're family. We only have each other."

"Yeah, you're right," Evan said, his voice calmer. "You know I'd do anything for you."

"You're the only one I trust," Stephan told him. "What's the issue, Evan?"

"Ashdown hired Hunter Black."

"Fuck," Stephan swore. Hunter Black was a pain in his ass. He'd been after him since his sister's death. Angie had worked for Stephan. She'd discovered something she shouldn't have, and he'd had to get rid of her. But Black had no reason to suspect he had something to do with her death.

"Exactly. Be very careful, Stephan. Let me take care of Jacinta. I'll get to her, I promise."

"I know you will, brother."

***

Jacey sat on the couch in their bedroom, watching the movie without really noticing what was on the screen. She jumped as she heard a creaking noise, her heart beating frantically before she realized it was just the wind.

She couldn't continue on like this, her nerves couldn't take it, not to mention the effect this was probably having on the baby. She had to do something to get rid of this threat over her head.

But so far she'd only come up with one plan, one she knew that Derrick would not be impressed with. But what other choice did they have?

She glanced over as the door to the bedroom opened, and Derrick stepped into the room. Instantly, her body went into overdrive, her clit tingling as her pussy clenched.

He raised an eyebrow as he saw her, his gaze running over her body. "Is that the way you should be dressed?"

Blushing, she stripped the large t-shirt off, leaving her completely naked.

"You're forgetting something else." He walked over to stand in front of her.

Jacey widened her thighs, exposing her pussy to his gaze.

"Good girl. Although if I have to remind you again, you'll be going over my knee."

She shivered at his words as he leaned down and gave her a scorching hot kiss.

"How was your day?" he asked as he sat next to her, drawing one of her legs over his. They were both facing the TV, although neither were paying the movie playing any attention.

"Fine," she said. "Boring. Just sitting around waiting for Evan and Stephan to make their move is driving me insane."

He glanced over at her in sympathy. "I know, baby girl. But there is little else we can do. It's too risky for you to leave the house right now."

His voice was tired, the lines around his eyes pronounced tonight and Jacey felt bad for complaining when he was obviously stressed out.

"I'm sorry, you're right. How was your day?"

He'd been working long hours lately, conducting most of his business by Skyping and conference calls to stay near the house.

"Not bad," he said, running his hand up and down her inner thigh, his fingertips brushing her pussy occasionally. "The resort in Rarotonga is coming along now, after a rather rocky start."

"Even though the locals think the site is haunted?" she asked, whimpering as he ran his fingertips over her labia, brushing against her clit.

"Hmm," he said distractedly as he used the remote to change the channel to the late night news. "In the beginning, we were having a hell of a time getting workers, but we've had the place blessed, and that seems to have helped."

Her breathing grew quicker as he continued to play with her pussy, swirling his fingers through her juices, twirling two fingers around her clit.

Orgasm flowed through her, swift and intense. Derrick simply pressed down on her clit, prolonging the pleasure until she'd drifted down from the high. Then he started all over again.

By the end of the news, she'd come five times, and he was working her up to a sixth when there was a knock on the door.

"Yeah?" he called out, his voice slightly hoarse.

"It's Hunter. We need to talk."

"Is it urgent?"

"No."

"Give me a minute." Derrick increased the speed of his fingers around her clit.

"I can't," she said in a whisper. Hunter was right outside the door. "What if he hears?"

"You'll have to be very quiet," he told her. "But you are going to come again.

He turned her, so she was lying on her back on the couch, one leg up on the back, the other falling off the side. Derrick dove between her legs, sucking on her clit, thrusting his fingers in and out of her passage until Jacey arched up, this orgasm even more intense than the last five, perhaps due to the secret thrill of knowing that Hunter was waiting for them on the other side of the door.

Derrick sat up, a grin on his face. He stood and helped her stand, turning her toward the bathroom.

"Go get yourself cleaned up."

Her head still in the clouds, she shuffled her way into the bathroom. Ten minutes later, Jacey had herself under some semblance of control. She wrapped her robe around her, then pushed open the bathroom door.

"We have to make a move," Hunter said. "We're getting nowhere like this. You can't live your lives in fear forever. Evan is out there watching. I know he is."

"Don't you think I know that?" Derrick replied, sounding uncharacteristically impatient. The strain of this was getting to him, and the guilt was eating at Jacey. "But we can't do anything that might risk Jacey's safety."

"We need to set a trap," Jacey interjected. Stepping into the room, she ignored Derrick's scowl as she walked over and sat on the sofa. Hunter was leaning back against the mantel above the fireplace, his arms folded across his massive chest.

"What sort of trap?" Hunter asked.

"I thought we could use me as bait to lure Evan out. Maybe I could drive somewhere, and once Evan was following I could lead him somewhere for you to grab him."

Derrick shook his head. "You've been watching too many crap cop shows," he told her. "One, no one is using you as bait, it's far too dangerous. And two, do you really think he's going to be stupid enough to fall for such a simple trap and how exactly would we trap him?"

"I figured Hunter would work out the details, he's the one with experience in this," she said surprised and a little put out by how he'd barrelled over her idea without even giving it some thought.

"Actually, it's similar to what I've been thinking," Hunter admitted.

"What?" Derrick said in a cold voice.

"Hear me out," Hunter replied, unfazed. "I said it was similar not the same. Evan's not stupid, but he thinks he's cleverer than he is. I think we should dress someone up like Jacey and send her with Derrick to that charity function coming up. Evan will think we're laying a trap. And he'll be right. It's just not the trap he thinks it is."

They both stared at him in confusion.

"Evan will think that we're using fake-Jacey as bait and that we'll have most of my men with Derrick and fake-Jacey, leaving the real Jacey here with minimal protection. He'll make a move on her, and we'll grab him."

"How does that not risk Jacey?" Derrick asked.

"Because we'll have removed Jacey to a safe house with Tiny and Connor."

Jacey thought it over, it sounded like it could work.

"No," Derrick said. "Absolutely not."

"Won't the security detail be stretched thin?" Jacey asked, ignoring Derrick's scowl. "I mean, if you have Tiny and Connor with me and supposedly a couple of guys watching Derrick in case he's not as smart as you think, who's left to grab Evan when he makes his move?"

"None of that matters because we're not doing this," Derrick insisted.

"I can call in some more men," Hunter replied. "But the main problem I have is that I don't have a female staff member to pretend to be Jacey."

"Wow, that surprises me," she said sarcastically. Hunter's views on women belonged in the nineteenth century.

"We need someone who is your build, who can look after themselves and who is willing to put themselves in a possibly dangerous situation. It would also help if they knew Austin well."

She thought for a long moment. "I might know someone. But I'll have to find her first."

"No. The two of you listen to me carefully. This is not happening." Derrick glared at them both.

"Let me work on him," Jacey told Hunter.

~

"You know he's right, don't you?" Jacey lay with her head on Derrick's chest in bed that night. She was exhausted. After Hunter had left, Derrick had picked her up, placed her on the bed and brought her to orgasm twice before taking her.

Derrick just grunted.

"We can't keep going like this, Derrick. I can't keep going like this. I'm jumping at every noise; I spend most of my days in fear. It's not good for the baby or for us. I think we have to try this."

"I don't like this. I don't like us being separated."

"I don't either. I particularly don't like the part where you're driving around, trying to get Evan to follow you. I hope Hunter's right, and he's too smart to fall for that. Maybe someone could pose as you as well. I couldn't stand it if anything happened to you, Derrick."

He scooted down until his head was level with her chest. "Nothing's going to happen to me. I'm more concerned about keeping you safe."

"Then give this a try. Please, Derrick."

He sighed, and she knew she had him.

He took a nipple into his mouth. Her leg rested on his hip, and he cupped her mound possessively.

She closed her eyes, exhaustion washing over her as he continued to suckle on her nipple.

This had to work. It just had to.

~

"Cady?"

Cady turned, her gaze darting around the dark street. There were few people around at this time of night. She took a defensive stance as she saw the large man bearing down on her. Her mind screamed run, but her body refused to cooperate.

"Who wants to know?" she asked suspiciously, trying to hide her fear.

"My name is Hunter Black. I run Black-Gray investigations. I'm currently working for Derrick Ashdown and Jacey Reynolds. I believe you know Jacey."

"Maybe," she replied, unwilling to admit anything. "What do you want?"

"I want you to work for me."

She snorted. "Yeah, right."

"Ms. Reynolds says you're smart, tough and can protect yourself. She said you'd been teaching her some self-defense. Can you shoot a gun?"

"Yes," she said.

"I need you for one night, to help us. Help Jacey. Will you do it?"

"How much are you paying?"

He smiled, and her heart stopped beating. Damn, he was gorgeous.

She had to be out of her mind to agree to anything he wanted.

"Three-fifty."

"Make it five hundred, and I want to talk to Jacey first." No way was she just trusting this man's word.

"I thought you would." He pulled out his phone and pressed something on the screen. "Here, please call her."

Reaching out, she took the phone from him, her fingers tingling where they touched his skin. Her breath caught, and she glanced up into his eyes, noticing the way they narrowed in interest.

Shit. She had a feeling she should have listened to her first instinct and fled the moment he said her name.

18

Derrick opened the bedroom door before picking up the tray laden with food that he'd placed on the floor. He stepped into the bedroom, swinging the door shut with his foot.

Jacey was sitting up in bed, the covers drawn up over her chest; she smiled over at him before putting down the e-reader he'd bought for her.

Over these last few weeks, he'd come to the realization that he loved her. He might have loved her from the first moment he'd met her. How could the love of a woman make him feel like he could do anything? Be anything? He wasn't sure, he only knew he was never going to let this feeling go.

"What's all this?" she asked as he placed the tray of food on the bedside drawers. He gave her a quick kiss before sitting, facing her.

"Tiny said you didn't eat dinner," he reprimanded gently.

She wrinkled her nose. "I'm not hungry."

Derrick placed a hand on her rounded stomach. "You know you need to eat. For yourself as well as the baby."

"I know. I just keep worrying about tomorrow night, and it ties my stomach up in knots until the thought of food is kind of nauseous."

Hunter had spoken to Cady a few days ago. After assessing her skill with a gun and her ability to defend herself, he'd given the plan they'd come up with the go-ahead for tomorrow night. Cady, pretending to be Jacey, would go with Derrick to a charity function while Jacey waited in a safe house with Connor and Tiny. Hunter and some of his team would be lying in wait for Evan to make a move on the house.

Damn, he hoped this worked.

"And that is why we're going to make a little game of this." He stood, grinning down at her. "Pull that blanket away."

"What? Why?" she asked in surprise.

"Now, Jacey," he said in his Dom voice. She immediately followed his order. Jacey was slowly coming to embrace her submissive side more and more. Her trust in him, in their relationship, was growing stronger each day.

Derrick walked over to the wardrobe where he kept some of his toys in a locked box.

"What are you doing?" she asked and he glanced over his shoulder to find her reclining back against the headboard, completely naked.

"I'm getting some toys. Want to see?"

She hesitated for a moment then nodded. He picked up the box then brought it over to the bed.

"I wondered what you kept in here," Jacey admitted.

"Been peeking?"

She blushed. "Maybe."

Derrick shook his head while she grinned at him.

"Show me, please," she said.

He unlocked the box and drew each item out, handing them to her. He watched her reactions carefully. Excitement flared in her eyes as he handed her the cuffs and rope he was going to use to tie her to the bed. The silken, red blindfold came next. Her breath quickened.

He drew out a vibrator with an attached clit tickler.

Jacey wrinkled her nose, keeping her hands on her lap.

Derrick raised a brow. "You don't want me to use this on you?"

"How many other women have you used it on?"

He chuckled. "No one, beautiful girl. It's brand new, bought just for you. I bought it at the same time that I bought this." He drew out a slim anal plug.

Her eyes widened as he handed her both the vibrator and the plug. The last thing he grabbed was a bottle of lube before he went to close the lid on the box.

"Wait, what else do you have in there?" she asked.

"Nothing you're ready for."

"I want to see," she said stubbornly.

"No."

"Derrick, please." She laid her hand on his. "I'm tired of being afraid. Show me."

"All right." He drew out a soft flogger and drew it over the smooth skin of her stomach. She sucked in her breath before relaxing as he just ran it over her skin in gentle circles.

"What else?" she asked.

He didn't keep a lot of toys at his home, preferring to do most of his playing at the club. But there was one more item left, a wooden paddle.

"Seriously? A paddle. Ouch. No. You're not using that on me."

Derrick put the paddle and the flogger back. "Not yet, anyway."

He placed the box on the floor, safely out of the way before turning back to her.

"Lean forward, baby." He put some pillows behind her back, making sure she was comfortable as she reclined back against them before securing her, her wrists and ankles cuffed and tied to each corner of the bed with long lengths of rope.

He tested the tightness of the cuffs, which were made of a soft, supple leather.

"How does that feel, beautiful? Any discomfit?" He hadn't stretched her legs and arms as wide apart as he could have. He wanted to ensure her comfort most of all.

"I'm good," she replied.

"Tell me if that changes. Right away."

"Yes, Sir."

Damn, he loved hearing her call him Sir.

He fixed the silk scarf over her eyes. "What's your safe word?"

"Pink, Sir."

"Good girl. Now, this is the way the game works. For every bite of food you eat, you get a reward."

Her breath caught. "And what if I don't eat it?"

"Then you get punished."

JESUS. What a choice, she kind of liked the sound of them both.

"Please me, baby, and I will please you," Derrick whispered in her ear.

She shivered in anticipation. Something cool passed her lips, and she opened them instinctively.

A grape. Yum.

"Very nice." Derrick kissed his way down her neck before placing another piece of food on her lips.

Some soft, buttered bread. As Jacey chewed, he continued to kiss down her body.

More food, more butterfly soft kisses that managed to avoid all the places she wanted him most. Her nipples, her pussy, her clit.

"Open wide." Another piece of bread touched her tongue, and Jacey chewed it for a long moment before swallowing. Derrick cupped her breasts.

"Please, Sir," she begged.

"What do you need, baby?"

"Touch my nipples, take them into your mouth, suck them."

"Well, you have been very good." He lightly tongued her distended nipples. Holding her breasts gently, knowing how tender they were, he moved from one nipple to the other. Jacey whimpered, her need spiralling out of control. She attempted to thrust her hips up, needing him to touch her clit, to drive himself inside her.

"Stay still," he ordered. "You still have some more food to finish."

He let her breasts go, and something else brushed her lips. Jacey turned her face away.

"No more, I need you."

"A little bit more and you'll get everything you need," he promised.

She opened her lips, allowing him to feed her. He parted her labia, brushing a finger against her clit. It was exquisite torture. Not nearly enough to send her crashing over the edge into bliss.

He stopped flicking her clit long enough to give her a drink of orange juice then his finger returned, this time with more pressure.

"Oh, oh, oh," she cried, her whole body on fire. It wouldn't take much, just a bit more...

Derrick pulled his finger away, and she cried out in protest.

"Derrick, no!"

He laughed. "We're going to have to work on your self-discipline. Next time, I'm going to order you to be quiet. What's the bet you end up with more punishment than pleasure?"

She trembled at his words. Self-discipline? She wasn't sure she liked the sound of that. She knew she would have definite problems with keeping silent.

"Just lie back, baby."

Two thick fingers pushed their way into her pussy, thrusting in and out before being replaced by the vibrator. Oh God, oh God. The vibrating tips surrounded her clit, and she gasped. Her whole body was swamped with need, bliss enveloping her. Orgasm swept over her, making her gasp for air, low whimpers filled the room as pulsated around the rubber shaft.

"Very nice. And again."

His fingers played with her nipple as he thrust the vibrator in and out of her in short, smooth strokes. The vibrating head brushed against that sensitive spot inside her and she could feel her orgasm growing, it rolled over her, lasting longer than the first one.

Her head dropped back in total relaxation as Derrick turned off the vibrator and drew it out of her pussy. He undid the cuffs on her ankles then wrists, massaging her arms.

Drawing her blindfold off, he took her mouth with his, sending scorching fire through her veins.

"How are you feeling, beautiful?" he asked.

"So good," she replied.

"Do you feel up to a bit more or do you need to rest?"

Oh, she definitely wanted more and so did he, if his erection was any indication.

"I want more."

He kissed her jaw. "Are you sure?"

"Derrick. I'm fine. Please, I need you inside me."

"On your hands and knees. Ass in the air. Head resting on your hands."

He helped her get into place. Anticipation sizzled through her as he parted her ass cheeks and dabbed some lube against her asshole.

"Just relax, Jacey." The lubed plug pressed against her hole and she took a deep breath, letting it out slowly as he pushed the plug deep inside her.

Derrick kissed one ass cheek then the other. He then smacked his hand down on each cheek.

"Ow, what was that for?"

"Just because I could," he replied.

He placed a hand between her legs, flicking his finger over her clit as two fingers of his other hand pumped in and out of her pussy.

The plug in her ass only added to her pleasure. When he finally lined his cock up with her pussy, pushing it bit by bit inside her, Jacey couldn't hold back her cries of delight.

"Bloody hell, that feels too good." He thrust in and out, driving inside her. "So damn tight."

He reached around and drew circles around her clit. Faster. Tighter. His thrusts became more powerful, both of them panting heavily, their bodies slick with sweat. "Come again for me, Jacey. I need you."

Those words sent her off into bliss. She barely heard his own yell of release as he came. Both of them collapsed on their sides, Derrick's arm still wrapped around her.

"I think you killed me," Derrick said. "I can't move."

"Ditto."

∼

"Promise me you'll be careful," Jacey said as Derrick hugged her tight against his chest.

"I promise," he told her. "You just promise me that you will do exactly as Tiny says. Because he'll be reporting back to me and you know what happens to girls who misbehave."

Her clit throbbed at his words.

"I will. I'll miss you." She and Tiny were about to sneak out of the house. It was close to two a.m. and pitch black outside. Connor was already in the car.

Tomorrow evening Derrick had an invitation to a charity function that he was going to pretend to attend with Cady at his side, pretending to be Jacey.

"Hopefully by this time tomorrow this nightmare will be over," she whispered.

"I love you, baby," he told her.

"I love you too."

He took her mouth with his, a scorching, all-encompassing kiss that had her gasping for breath when he released her.

There was a knock on the bedroom door.

"Jacey. Time," Tiny said through the door. There were no lights on as they didn't want to alert Evan to what they were doing. But Derrick managed to guide her over to the door without either of them tripping.

"Look after my girl, Tiny," Derrick said as he gave her one last hug.

"I will."

∼

Jacey lay on the lumpy bed in the safe house, knowing she wasn't going to be able to go back to sleep. She looked over at the clock on the nightstand.

3:37 a.m.

Their exit from the house and trip to the safe house had gone smoothly. When they'd arrived, Tiny had shown her to her room. She'd promptly collapsed on the bed in exhaustion.

She should sleep. She needed to sleep. But there was no way it was coming to her while she knew Derrick was still in danger.

She pulled out her phone and sent him a quick text.

ALL GOOD. *Luv u.*

LESS THAN A MINUTE LATER, her phone buzzed.

LUV U 2. Get some sleep!

BOSSY BASTARD. But a grin was on her face as she closed her eyes and did her best to let sleep take over.

～

8.35 P.M.

Jacey paced across the living room floor. Derrick would have left the house by now, heading toward the charity function that started at nine.

"You're distracting me with all your pacing," Connor complained. "I'm tracking them now, everything is fine."

He'd obviously never had anyone he loved in danger. Everything would not be *fine* until she could see Derrick was safe with her own two eyes.

"He's just pulling into the parking lot now," Connor said into a microphone. "And they're inside and safe."

"How do we know it's safe?" Jacey asked. "What if Evan has someone planted inside?"

"So do we," Tiny replied. "He's safe."

"What about the house? Has there been any movement?" she asked.

"Nothing," Connor said, he'd set things up so he could monitor the house security from the safe house. "But it's early yet."

Jacey heard her cell ringing in her bedroom. "I'll be back in a minute." Her heart was beating wildly, hoping it was Derrick but knowing he probably wouldn't risk calling her.

She checked the name displayed.

Holly.

"Hey, Holly, what's up?" she asked, trying to keep the worry from her voice.

"Jacey? Are you alone? Can anyone hear you?" Holly asked, sounding upset.

"Holly? What is it? Are you okay?" Jacey asked in worry.

"Are you alone?" Holly insisted.

"Yes, tell me what's wrong."

"Jacey, I'm so sorry. He said if I didn't call you that he'd kill Brax. I'm so sorry."

A chilling calm came over Jacey. This is the one thing they hadn't factored in to their plan. That Evan might outmanoeuvre them all.

"Holly, it's okay. Where are you? What has he–"

Some shuffling noises and a low, pain-filled cry filled the phone. Then the voice she heard in her nightmares came across the phone.

"Hello, sister."

"I'm not your sister, Evan. What have you done to Holly and Brax? If you've hurt them–"

His chilling laughter came through the phone.

"You'll do what? Stomp your feet and cry? Call for your boyfriend and his friends to save you? That would be a very bad mistake, Jacinta, or should I call you Jacey? Because the minute any of your friends turn up, I'm going to shoot the lovely Holly, and you wouldn't want that, would you?"

"No," she said, fear making her teeth chatter. "What do you want?"

"You're going to come to the following address. Alone. Tell anyone and Holly dies, understand me?"

"What about Brax?"

"Oh, I think he's pretty much dead."

A muffled scream came from the background, the sound haunting in its sorrow.

Tears filled Jacey's eyes. She'd done this. By wanting something for herself, she had selfishly brought this monster into their lives. Brax's death was her fault.

She had to save Holly.

"Where do you want me to go?"

He named an address that was right across town. She had no idea how Evan had found Holly and Brax and right now that didn't matter.

"You have one hour to get here. And remember to come alone."

∽

JACEY DREW out the credit card Derrick had given her with shaking hands and handed it to the taxi driver.

"You sure you want to be dropped off here, miss?" the older taxi driver asked kindly.

The area didn't look all that appealing. There were a lot of large, empty, rundown buildings and very little lighting. She swallowed heavily. She didn't have time to be afraid.

"I'm sure. Thank you."

She took back the credit card and placed it in her pocket before climbing out of the taxi.

Her hand fiddling with her necklace, she walked toward the address Evan had given her. Dragging open the sliding door of the derelict warehouse, Jacey tried to calm her racing heartbeat, the need to run was almost overwhelming. But she forced herself to piece together some courage and stepped further into the building.

A lone light flicked on, and she was face to face with a man she had hoped to never see again.

"Hello, Jacinta."

"Where is Holly?" she asked, trying to keep the tremors from her voice.

"Oh, she's someplace safe."

She scowled. "Where? You said she would be here."

"No, I said I'd kill her if you didn't come alone. Don't worry, she's closely watched. Do as I tell you and I won't have to kill her. Disobey me and all it will take is one phone call and..." He slashed a finger across his throat.

"How do I know you haven't killed her already?" she asked.

Evan pulled a phone out of his pocket and pressed his thumb down on the screen.

"Hello?"

"Put the woman on," Evan ordered.

"Hello? Hello?"

Jacey slumped in relief as Holly's voice came across the phone.

"Holly, are you okay?"

"Jacey, I—"

Evan shut the conversation off before Holly could say any more.

"Do you plan on killing me here?" she asked Evan.

"That was the original plan. However, having you turn up with a bullet in your brain in some warehouse in Austin isn't going to be easily explained. No, we need your death to be a nice little accident, well, to look like one anyway. So you and I are going to take a drive."

Christ, where was Tiny? She hadn't been stupid enough to leave the safe house without telling Tiny and Connor about the phone call. Even if she'd made it out of the house without alerting them, it would have been suicide to come here alone.

And Jacey wasn't ready to die yet. She had too much to live for. She placed her hand over her belly protectively as Evan grabbed her with his free hand, his other hand clutching a gun.

Tiny would follow her and Connor was tracking her. Before leaving the safe house, Connor had told her about the GPS in her necklace. Apparently, Derrick, the sneaky bastard, had put a tracking device on her necklace without telling her. Tiny and Connor would find her.

Whether she would be alive or dead was going to be up to her.

~

"What the hell do you mean, Evan has Jacey?" Derrick roared, glaring at Connor who was ignoring him, his whole attention on the computer screen in front of him.

When he'd received a call from Hunter, he'd driven over to the safe house like a maniac. Cady had jumped in the car with him, demanding to know what was wrong.

"How the hell did he get to her?" he demanded.

"He kidnapped your sister-in-law and her husband," Hunter explained. "Used them as bait to lure Jacey out. She wasn't stupid, she took Tiny as back-up."

"So how is it that she's now in a car with Evan?" Derrick shouted.

"Evan moved quickly. Tiny was scouting the area when Evan shoved her in a car. He's following them," Connor said. "I'm tracking her necklace."

Thank Christ he'd had the foresight to put a tracking device on her necklace.

"Have you tracked Holly's necklace?" he demanded. He'd sent a similar necklace to his sister-in-law and Ava at their men's requests.

Connor nodded. "Gray took some of our men over to where the signal is coming from."

"Jaron, you're with me," Hunter ordered. "They already have a head start. Connor, keep us updated on their location."

Derrick followed them out.

"Derrick, it would be better if you stayed here," Hunter said, not without sympathy.

"Like fuck," Derrick replied. "I'm coming as well. Besides, my phone already has the program on it to track her. It'll be quicker than relying on Connor."

"I'm coming too," Cady said, crossing her arms over her chest as they all turned to glare at her. "What? She's my friend."

"I need you here with Connor," Hunter told her. "You stay on the phone with us while he works."

"No."

Hunter took a step toward her, looming over her. She swallowed heavily but didn't step away.

"You're staying. In case you forgot, sweetheart, I'm your boss for the night, and you do as I say. Jaron, Derrick, let's go."

Cady didn't say anything more, just spun away.

Derrick climbed into the front passenger seat. He was furious. How dare she place herself in danger this way? When he had her back safe, and well in his arms he was going to beat her ass until she couldn't sit down for a week.

∼

"Where are we going?" Jacey asked, staring out the window as they drove further away from the city. They'd been driving for two hours now, and the houses had become few and far between.

She hoped like hell that Tiny wasn't far behind them. She didn't dare look behind her, not wanting to alert Evan.

"Do you know that your old college friend, Suzy, has a ranch out here?" Evan said.

Jacey frowned. "No. What has that got to do with anything? I haven't seen Suzy in years." In fact, they hadn't really been friends. Suzy's mother and her mother had been close.

"The last couple of years have been hard on the ranch; they've lost a lot of money and are near foreclosure. Something I'm sure you understand Suzy finds very humiliating."

Suzy had always cared about appearances more than anything else.

"So she was very grateful for a little injection of cash. And all she has to do is corroborate Stephan's story that you've been staying with her since you returned from Europe, that's where he's been telling people you are. You borrowed this car from her to drive into Austin then on the way home; tragically, you had an accident, drove off the road, into the river and drowned."

"This is absurd. There are so many holes in that story it's laughable. There is no way anyone will believe it. And are you forgetting Derrick?"

"Don't worry about Derrick. We have plans for him. And I find that people often believe what they want to believe. Stephan has a lot of friends and people who owe him favors. I think you'll find that those holes are quickly filled in.

Jacey shivered. *Please hurry up, Tiny. Please.*

"And here we are, the place of your demise." He slowed the car to a stop but didn't turn it off, leaving the headlights on.

"I'm going to get out of the car. Don't try anything funny. Remember Holly."

"Not a lot I can do is there?" She nodded her head to where he'd cuffed her hands to the door handle.

"No," he said with a chuckle. "I suppose not."

Evan came around and opened her door, forcing her arms out in front of her. She would have fallen if the seatbelt hadn't caught her. He had the keys to her cuffs, and she wasn't going anywhere while attached to the door.

So she bided her time as he unlocked her cuffs.

"Undo your belt and get out," he demanded, keeping the gun pointed at her.

She climbed out slowly.

"Now, you're going to be a good little girl and climb in the driver's side then drive this car full speed over the edge. The water is cold and deep, not that you're going to survive the drop."

"And what makes you think I'll willingly drive off the road? Why wouldn't I just get in the car and drive away?"

Why was she telling him this? Why didn't she just do it?

"Because if you don't, then it's bye-bye Holly. You're a do-gooder,

Jacinta, always have been. We both know you're not going to risk her life to save your own."

He was right. Luckily, she was pretty sure she didn't have to.

"Ahh, but do you really have Holly? Because I'm thinking that right about now, she's been rescued." God, she hoped so.

"Nice try."

"Why don't you call and find out?"

He shoved her away from him, stepping back with his gun firmly trained on her as he reached into his pocket for his cell. The phone rang and rang.

No answer.

"Well, never mind, I don't need your cooperation to knock you out and push you into the water."

He started to move toward her, and she knew he was serious. Even though it took her closer to the edge of the road, Jacey matched him step for step, moving away from him.

"Freeze! Put your hands up." *Tiny.*

Relief made her so weak, she nearly fell to her knees. Evan spun around, and she took the opportunity to dive around the other side of the car.

"Who's there? Jacinta, come back here, you bitch!" There was the ping of bullets against the car, and she crouched down further. Shoot! She was a sitting duck here.

"Jacey, stay down!" Tiny roared.

"I'm going to kill you, Jacinta!" Evan sounded insane. He didn't even seem to be aware of Tiny anymore. There was the sound of a gun firing then a scream of outrage. She raised her head far enough to see Evan grab at his shoulder. He stepped backward, once, twice then fell over the barrier into the river below.

His scream of outrage reverberated throughout the night, and Jacey heaved in huge breaths, unable to calm her raging heartbeat.

There was the sound of running footsteps, and she turned, sagging in relief as she saw Tiny race toward her.

"Oh God, oh God," she said, trying to force herself to stand but her legs seemed to be made of rubber. "Do you think he's dead?" she asked as Tiny crouched in front of her.

He hauled her up into his arms.

"Don't know. Too dark." He carried her away from the car.

"You saved me. Thank you." Tears filled her eyes, rolling down her cheeks. She was all over the place. She couldn't even stand, let alone walk and she couldn't seem to stop crying.

"I was almost too late."

"What about the car? We can't just leave it there."

"The others are coming."

Headlights appeared in the distance. Jacey started to sob as car doors slammed and she heard Derrick yell her name. The next moment he was there, pulling her from Tiny's arms and hugging her tightly against his chest.

"Thank God. Thank God. You are never leaving my sight again, understand me? Even if I have to chain you to me."

At the moment, she couldn't agree with that sentiment more.

"I love you, Jacey."

"I love you, too."

19

Jacey stood in the open doorway of their bungalow, looking out at the glistening sea of Muri Beach. Two arms surrounded her from behind, cupping her round belly.

"What are you thinking about, love?" Derrick asked.

"Just how much I'm going to miss this place. It's been idyllic, staying here." It was a slower pace of life on Rarotonga. Here, people moved at their own speed. Island time, they called it.

"We'll come back. I promise."

"I know." She leaned her head back against his chest. "I guess I just managed to push everything out of my mind while we were here and now..."

"Now you're worrying about Stephan's trial."

She nodded. Even with Evan gone, she was still in danger. Stephan had enough money to hire someone else to come after her. There had been nothing to connect Stephan with Evan's actions, no paperwork, no emails.

Nothing except her.

Either she spent the rest of her life hiding from him, or she went public with what she knew. So with Derrick's support, Jacey had gone to the police with what she knew about Gerry's death.

Stephan had been granted bail, and she was terrified he'd find some way to hurt her. Or Derrick. Knowing how stressed she was, Derrick decided to bring her to Rarotonga for a vacation. It also gave him a chance to check up on the resort his company was building.

"Don't worry. I have security watching you and the house. You'll be safe."

"I just don't want to live like this for the rest of my life."

"You won't. The bastard is going down. Come on, we have one more night left. Let me take your mind off everything."

Jacey let Derrick draw her back into the hut.

∼

JACEY WAS SITTING beside Derrick in a private lounge in LAX while Derrick's jet refilled. She glanced up from her magazine to look at the television screen as a news bulletin came on. She grabbed Derrick's arm.

Derrick turned to her. "What is it?"

"Look," she said, raising a shaking hand to point at the TV screen that was showing some news footage of Stephan from a few years ago. Derrick stood and grabbed an attendant who turned the volume up.

"For those of you who have just joined us. It has just been confirmed that Stephan Worthington, disgraced state district attorney for Chicago committed suicide last night. He was found this morning by his lawyer. Mr. Worthington was on bail after being arrested for the murder of his assistant, Gerald Francis. During the investigation into this alleged murder, it has been found that Mr. Worthington, who comes from one of Chicago's most prestigious families, has been embezzling funds and taking bribes during his period as state district attorney."

"Come away, baby. You've heard enough. The plane should be ready by now."

Jacey let Derrick steer her away in a daze. She followed him through the airport, not really taking notice of her surroundings as Derrick helped her onto the plane and settled her in her seat.

"I can't believe that Stephan would commit suicide. He was always so confident; I never thought he would take his own life."

Derrick did up her seat belt before doing up his own. He glanced down at her in concern. "This wasn't your fault, Jacey. He did some evil things, maybe his conscience caught up with him."

"Maybe. And he was embezzling funds? Taking bribes? Why? He had plenty of money."

Derrick shrugged. "It was probably about power."

"They discovered all of this quickly."

"I think Hunter and his team may have helped with that. Connor has been doing some research."

"Oh." Her mind reeled. "I still can't believe he would take his own life." She turned to him in shock. "Why would he do that?"

Derrick tucked her into his side. "I don't know. Maybe because he knew he was losing everything and he just couldn't face it."

The loss of his job, his social standing would be a huge blow to someone like Stephan, but she'd still never imagined him killing himself.

"Come on, let's get you home."

She let Derrick steer her through the airport and outside to where Robert waited with the car.

Home sounded really good right now.

~

"I got a thank you card today." Jacey closed her laptop and looked over at Derrick, who was working on a new project. She lay back on the couch. "Apparently a large donation was made in my name to the Downtown Mission shelter."

Derrick looked up at her. "That so?"

"Hmm, they were very happy with my generosity." The smile slipped from her face, and she looked at him seriously. "Thank you, Derrick."

He nodded. "It was the very least I could do." He sat back in his seat.

"You know that you're going to have to let me out of your sight at some stage and go back to work."

Since returning from Rarotonga, Derrick had been working from home. He'd become even more overprotective and she'd been happy to indulge him. He'd nearly lost her, and she knew that had stirred up old nightmares of when his wife died. Derrick was always going to be overprotective and bossy; truthfully, she wouldn't have him any other way.

But there was a limit as to how much she'd take from him, and it was time to get back some of her independence.

"I know," he said sitting back in his seat, running his gaze over her body. "Lift up your skirt and spread your legs."

"Derrick, you're working."

He raised a brow. "Not anymore. I've taken the rest of the day off. I have a naughty little subbie to punish. This has been a long time coming."

"What? Why? What did I do?"

"What did you do?" he asked darkly. "Let's see. You left the safe house where you promised me you would stay. You put yourself in grave danger, not only risking yourself but also our baby, and you added a whole pile of gray hairs to my head."

She snorted at that last one.

"Now raise that skirt and spread your legs."

She slowly did as he ordered. Derrick didn't allow her to wear underwear in the house so he could see every inch of her exposed pussy.

His phone rang, and he looked over at the display. "I have to take this. You stay just as you are."

The entire time he was talking on the phone, he stared at her, his gaze drinking her in. How he was able to concentrate, she didn't know because her mind was a scattered mess.

When he put down his phone, he gestured to her. "Come here."

She slowly stood and walked toward him.

"Strip."

She'd grown much larger now, her belly quite prominent and her breasts fuller. She pulled off her shirt, putting it aside, then her bra. Finally, she pulled down her skirt.

"Have I told you how beautiful you are lately?"

She grinned. "Only a few times."

He ran his hand over her stomach possessively. Then leaning in, he kissed her belly.

"You've been a very naughty girl, haven't you?" he asked.

"Yes, Sir."

"How should I punish you?"

"I-I suppose you could spank me, Sir?" she said with mock-reluctance.

"Yes, I suppose that would teach you a lesson. Ask me to punish you," Derrick demanded as he stood.

"Please, Sir. Spank me."

"Since you asked so nicely. You will grasp the edge of the desk and bend over."

He smacked his hand down on her thigh. "You know better than that, I want those legs spread wide."

"Sorry, Sir."

"You're not yet. But you will be."

He spanked her fast and hard. Tears filled her eyes. She knew he held back, though. Knew her pregnancy made him take extra care.

He stopped, rubbing her buttocks.

"How are you?" he asked.

"Good, Sir."

He pushed two fingers into her pussy which was wet and welcoming.

"Ahh, yes, I can see that." He swirled a finger around her clit, slowly at first then faster.

"Why are you being punished?"

"For endangering myself and the baby," she answered, her breath coming in fast pants as he stroked her toward orgasm. Abruptly he pulled away.

She heard a creaking as he sat on the chair.

"Come and thank me for your punishment," he ordered.

She turned to find him sitting in the chair, his trousers undone, his hand massaging his firm cock. Knowing what he wanted, Jacey knelt between his open thighs and took his cock in her mouth, sucking him down. She played with his balls, knowing exactly what he liked as she sucked him further down her throat.

"Faster. Harder."

She bobbed her head up and down, sucking on him as hard as she could until, with a guttural groan, he came in her mouth. She drank all of him, licking at his shaft as it softened slightly, poking the tip of her tongue into his slit.

Derrick drew her up onto his lap and kissed her.

"Very good. Now, how about some dinner? I don't know about you, but I'm starving."

He set her on her feet then stood and did up his pants.

"B-but," she spluttered, her body humming with arousal.

"But what?" he asked with pretended ignorance, his eyes dancing. "You aren't hungry? You have to eat, little girl." He patted her stomach gently.

Jacey bit back her growl of disbelief. *Obviously, her punishment wasn't quite over.* She followed him out of the study and into the kitchen.

"Up you go." He lifted her onto the breakfast counter.

"Derrick, what are you doing?" she asked as her bottom hit the cold granite.

"I want something pretty to look at while I'm cooking our dinner," he explained. "Lie back, arms above your head, put your feet up on the granite and spread your legs."

"Derrick!"

"What do you call me?" he asked sternly.

"Sir."

"Now do as you were told."

Jacey lay back, putting her arms up and spreading her legs wide. Derrick stared at her for a long moment then shook his head.

"You're going to get uncomfortable like that." He helped her sit up, so her legs were dangling over the edge.

"Legs spread and place your hands on your thighs. Tell me if you get uncomfortable," he ordered sternly.

She nodded, feeling breathless with anticipation.

As he walked past to get something, he would stop and caress her pussy, sometimes suck her clit or tweak a nipple. By the time he'd finished cooking dinner, her body was on fire, and she thought she might explode. But as he led her to the dining room, she had the feeling things were only just beginning.

DERRICK FED Jacey her dinner as she sat next to him, her legs spread wide. He'd turned their chairs so they were facing one another and he could see every exposed inch of her.

Her nipples were hard and rosy red, her pussy lips swollen and wet with her dew. Fire sparked from her eyes as she stared at him. He knew she needed to come.

But she needed to know how badly she'd scared him and that it was totally unacceptable to him for her to put herself in danger. The spanking was the hardest he'd ever given her, but it still wasn't enough.

"Tell me why you're being punished again," he asked.

With a small frown, she replied, "Because I put myself and the baby in danger."

"Do you know why I'm so angry about that?" he asked as he cupped her breasts, playing with her nipples.

"Be-because you love me," she said, her breath coming faster, her eyes half-lidded with her desire.

"Because I cannot live without you. If you'd died, part of me would have too. I don't think I could go on living without you, Jacey."

Her eyes widened.

"But I didn't die."

"You could have. It will take me a long, long time before I ever forget that. If I ever do."

"And have you forgiven me for it?" she asked.

"Not quite yet," he told her. "That's what tonight is for. Go into the living room and wait for me. I want you on all fours on the sofa, with your forehead resting on your wrists."

She nodded and immediately rose. He watched her butt sway as she walked toward out of the dining room. Every day he thanked God that nothing had happened to her and every night he still woke up in sweat with nightmares. He knew he had to get past this. He might not ever forget, but he had to find some way of working through this.

Otherwise, he really might have to chain her to his side as he'd threatened.

JACEY GROANED as he spread her ass cheeks wide and drove a finger deep into her asshole. He'd been playing with her for the last half-hour; although it seemed like much longer, teasing her nipples, flicking her clit, finger-fucking her asshole. If she didn't come soon, then she was going to explode. He now had her splayed on her back on the sofa, her legs spread, her hands beneath her head as he stroked her body to near orgasm time and time again.

She'd sucked him off twice, and he was hard yet again.

He pushed another finger inside her, thrusting them in and out quickly, making her whole body shiver.

"Please, Sir, please. I promise I will never do it again."

"Never do what?" he asked.

"Never put myself in danger."

"Damn right you won't. Shit. I have to have you. I need to be inside you." He squirted some lube on his hand then rubbed it over his cock. She didn't know where the lube had come from, although it wouldn't surprise her if he had some stuck in drawers around the house.

"On your knees, beautiful. Rest your arms against the arm of the sofa."

He helped her move slowly into position.

"Relax, Jacey."

He spread her cheeks and pushed his cock into her asshole.

"Oh God, that feels so good."

Jacey murmured her agreement her head dropping forward. This wasn't something she'd ever thought she'd enjoy after the way Stephan had used her, but the feel of Derrick's cock pushing inside her, filling her... it was bliss.

Reaching around, Derrick flicked her clit, rubbing it.

"Ohh."

"Come when you want, don't hold back."

It didn't take much, a few thrusts of his cock, his fingers manipulating her clit before she was shuddering her way through an overwhelming orgasm.

"You feel so hot. Come again for me, baby."

He reached around and rubbed her nipples. She groaned feeling the sensation all the way down to her clit.

"Sir, Sir, more."

Leaving her breasts, he thrust two fingers deep into her pussy, driving them in as he played with her clit with the fingers of her other hand.

"I'm going to come!" she cried.

He continued to thrust deep inside her, the dual sensation of his cock in her ass and his fingers deep in her pussy made her scream as she came again. Derrick rocked inside her, letting out his own shout of release as he came.

∽

AN HOUR LATER, after they'd cleaned up and moved into the bedroom, Jacey lay snuggled up to him in bed. Derrick ran his hand up and down her back.

"So, does this mean you've forgiven me?"

His hand stilled. "Yes." He grasped hold of her chin gently, raising her face. "But you will never, ever do something like this again, understand me?"

"Yes, Sir," she replied. "I promise."

She ran her hand over his chest. "Do you think Holly is going to come back to work for you?"

Derrick sighed and put his hands behind his head. "I don't know. Truthfully, I don't think she will. The experience was extremely traumatic for her. I'm just so bloody thankful that Brax didn't die."

It had been a close call. Brax had been shot in the chest, but thankfully it hadn't been close to his heart. He'd recently been released from the hospital and was back home with Holly looking after him. But they'd all been worried about Holly. She'd been traumatized by what happened, particularly from nearly losing Brax. She'd run herself down to the point of exhaustion in the hospital until Derrick had stepped in.

"So you'll hire someone in the meantime."

"Yes."

"Think you can find anyone who will put up with you?" Jacey teased.

"Well," he said, rolling her over onto her other side and spreading her legs. He slipped inside her from behind. Jacey gasped at the sensation. "I guess I thought I'd already found her."

"Me? You want me to work for you? Do you think that's a good idea?"

"Temporarily. We could see how it goes. I'm not quite ready to let you out of my sight, Jacey, and I do need some help. What do you say?"

He'd increased his pace, his hand slipping around her body to play with her clit.

"Say you'll help me."

"You don't exactly fight fair, you know," she replied, her voice growing breathless.

"I'd never win if I did that. And I like to win."

She snorted, her hips rising to meet his thrusts.

"You'll start working on your overprotective issues. I'm not made of glass. Nothing is going to happen to me."

He thrust deeper, faster. "Always going to watch out for you. It's who I am. But I'll try to give you more space. Maybe."

Well, she supposed that was a start. Of sorts.

"So you'll do it?"

"Yes. But I'm not putting up with any funny stuff. Things will be strictly business at the office. No more telling me to raise my skirt and spread my legs."

"We'll see."

Printed in Great Britain
by Amazon